# The Boy on the Beach

*For Jenny*

# The Boy
# on the Beach

By Margaret Meacham

Illustrations by Marcy Dunn Ramsey

Tidewater Publishers

Centreville, Maryland

Library of Congress Cataloging-in-Publication Data

Meacham, Margaret
    The boy on the beach  /  by Margaret Meacham  ;  illustrations by
Marcy Dunn Ramsey. — 1st ed.
        p.    cm.
    Summary:  Thirteen-year-old Jessie and her younger brother find a
strange boy on the beach, who claims to have traveled forward in
time from 1892 and needs their help in retrieving his time travel
device.
    ISBN  0-87033-441-7  (pbk.)
    [1. Time travel—Fiction. 2. Science fiction.]    I. Ramsey, Marcy
Dunn, ill.  II. Title.
PZ7.M47886Bo    1992
[Fic]—dc20                                                92-23975
                                                              CIP
                                                              AC

Manufactured in the United States of America
First edition

# 1

THIS MORNING, as I was pawing through the junk in my closet looking for my left running shoe, the brown paper bag with Reuben's clothes in it fell off my closet shelf. Its contents spilled out into the mess of shoes, belts, hair ribbons, and tote bags, and there they lay like artifacts from a museum: the black knickers, the oilskin rain gear, the heavy lace-up boots, all that we have left of him. I sat there staring at his things and thinking about the day we found him and I decided that I had to write it all down.

Since I was already late for school, I couldn't start right then, but I've been thinking about it all day. Now I'm in study hall, and I'm finally able to begin writing. I see that Ms. Glick, our study hall teacher, is looking at me, making sure I'm busy. Ms. Glick tends to get irritated if you don't look busy during study hall. You can tell when she's getting irritated because she starts making this clicking noise with her pencil known as the Glick click. She clicks louder and louder and louder, and then she starts in with her foot. By the time she finally gets up to walk over to your desk to say, "Don't you have work to do?" she's making so much noise with her clicking that no one can get any work done anyway.

Ms. Glick must have decided we're all sufficiently busy because she's now applying fresh lipstick—bright red, of course. You know those red wax lips that turn into chewing gum? Well, Ms. Glick's lips could have been the model for those. I'm not kidding. They're the biggest lips I've ever seen. And she's got these tiny little eyes that blink a lot. To give you the big picture, she looks a lot like my little brother's hamster would look if he were wearing a hamster-sized pair of wax lips.

But I digress. That's what our math teacher always says when she finally realizes that we've succeeded in using up half the period by talking about what it was like to be a civil rights demonstrator in the sixties instead of about algebra.

Getting back to the story, I guess I should start with the day we found him. Reuben, I mean, although we didn't know that was his name back then. It was just a few weeks ago, but it seems like centuries have passed since then.

It was late on a Friday afternoon, the end of a long, lousy week. It was really warm for the end of September. Hot, almost. Indian summer, Mom calls it. When I got home from school, Will (that's my little brother—he's six, seven years younger than me) begged me to take him down to the beach. Since there was nothing better to do, I decided I might as well. We had gone wading, and then I had sat down on the sand by the water's edge, letting the waves wash over my feet, and Will had wandered up the beach, playing Ninja Turtles. I don't know how long I sat there, but I know it was a while, because the sun was getting lower in the sky, and my hair was beginning to frizz up into those stiff salty wisps that remind me of the scarecrow in *The Wizard of Oz*. I was trying to remember whether the scarecrow had wanted a heart or a brain—I can never remember which it was—when I heard Will.

"Jessie! Jessie!" he shouted, racing up the beach toward me.

I stood up. Something had frightened him. I could hear it in his voice and see it in the way he ran. When he got to me he grabbed my arm and began pulling me back up the beach from where he had come.

"Whoa. What's wrong, Willy?" I asked him.

"Come on. You have to come and see. He—he's hurt. He's got a big hurt on his head." He kept pulling at me until I finally took his hand and followed him.

"Who? Who has a hurt?" I asked.

"Come on. You'll see," he said. He led me up the beach and into the reeds. Then he stopped and pointed, and that's when I first saw him. I'll never forget that moment, the way we both just stood there, me with my hand over my mouth and Will with his arm extended, as though we had both been frozen in time. Finally I took a few steps closer.

THE BOY ON THE BEACH

There in the reeds between the beach and the woods was a boy. He lay on his back, his arms at his sides. His eyes were closed, and his head was turned to one side. An ugly red gash, three or four inches long, ran from just above his right eye and across his temple to his ear. He wore a brown slicker and heavy rubber boots that laced up almost to his knees. It was a weird outfit, one that none of the guys I knew would be caught dead wearing (oops . . . sorry . . . I guess that's not the best phrase to choose under the circumstances), but at the time I wasn't paying much attention to what he was wearing. It was the gash that caught my attention. It was horrible, caked with dried blood; and the skin around it was swollen and purple. It made me sick to look at it, but I couldn't help looking—like when you pass an accident on the road, and you don't want to look but you can't help it.

"We shouldn't move him," I told Will, "In my first aid class they said you should never move an injured person."

"Is he . . . is he breathing?" Will asked.

"I don't know."

I didn't want to get any closer, but I had to find out if he was alive or . . . the alternative. I have never seen a dead person, and I'll tell you, I hope I never do see one. It was bad enough seeing someone that close to being dead. I knelt down beside him and reached out to touch his hand. My fingers were trembling so badly I could hardly control them. His hand felt warm, and I pressed my fingers against the inside of his wrist.

"He has a pulse. He's alive," I told Will, and I saw the relief that I felt mirrored in his eyes.

"What's that in his other hand?" Will asked.

It was a round gold object attached to a gold chain. "I don't know. It looks like a pocket watch or something," I said. "We better not touch it. We've got to get help, Will. Come on. Let's get Mom. Quickly."

I stood up and grabbed Will's hand and we ran up the path that leads through the reeds to our backyard. I ran faster than I've ever run in my life, half-pulling, half-carrying Will. My heart was pounding and my lungs ached and I felt as if I could hardly breathe, but when we got to our yard I began to scream for Mom over and over, and she came running out of the house.

"Jessie, honey. What is it?"

Then I was in Mom's arms and sobbing like a little kid, while Will just stood there beside us, his eyes huge in his silent face. It was weird. I don't know why I reacted that way, but I guess it was the shock. All of a sudden I was acting like a two-year-old, and there was Will, not even crying. Mom held me for a minute and then said, "What is it, honey? What happened?"

"Oh, Mom. He's on the beach. He's got this horrible cut on his forehead. I . . . I thought he was dead, but he's not. He's got a pulse. He's not dead."

"Whoa, whoa. Slow down, Jess," Mom said, putting her hands on my shoulders. "Catch your breath and then let's start from the beginning."

Then we told her about how Will had found him and about the gash on his head.

"Oh my," said Mom. She stood with her chin in her hand the way she always does when she's trying to decide what to do. "Should I come down and have a look at him, or should we call an ambulance right away?"

"I think we should call someone, Mom. We don't know how bad it is," I said.

Mom looked at me closely and then nodded. "Okay. I'll go right in and call."

Will and I followed her into the house and she went to the phone and dialed the emergency number.

"Yes. An emergency," she said into the phone. "A boy has been injured. A head injury, we think. No. No relation. We don't even know him. My daughter found him on the beach near our house. No, we know nothing about him. He's—just a minute." She looked over at me. "How old would you say he is, Jess?"

"About my age, I guess," I told her. "Or maybe a year older. It's kind of hard to tell, but I'd say thirteen or fourteen. Right, Will?"

Will nodded, and Mom went back to the phone. "About thirteen, we think. Yes. Yes, I'll be waiting here for them. That's 47 Cedar Road. Yes. Thank you." Mom hung up and looked at me. "Okay. Why don't you take a blanket down and cover him up. It might not help, but at least we'll feel like we're doing something for him. Will and I will sit here until the ambulance comes." She pulled our old picnic blanket down from the shelf in the hall closet and handed it to me, and I headed back down to the beach.

By this time it was past six. The sun was getting ready to sink into the river, and I could tell there was going to be a great sunset. The clouds were feathery and fringing the horizon, already turning into a collage of pinks and purples. As I walked up the beach I watched an osprey as it circled and dove into the river after a fish. For a minute it seemed like an ordinary evening, but when I came to the spot where he lay I knew it was no ordinary evening. I knew as I stood looking down at him that I would be seeing more of him, and that something important was going to happen. I don't know how I knew that or why, but I do know that I felt it.

As I drew the blanket up over his arms I noticed that the gold thing he had been holding was gone. His hand lay empty and open at his side, and there was no sign of it. I looked around in the sand nearby, but it was gone. Weird, I thought. What could have happened to it? It couldn't have just disappeared. Had someone taken it?

I sat down on a nearby piece of driftwood to wait for Mom and the men from the ambulance. I looked at his face. It was hard to tell exactly what he looked like because of the wound, and because his eyes were closed, but all in all I thought it looked like a pretty nice face. Where had he come from, I wondered, and why was he wearing those dorky clothes? The boots looked like something my grandfather might wear, and the slicker, well, the last time

I had seen one like it was in the movie *Moby Dick,* the one about the old dude who's obsessed with capturing the white whale. Why would a kid be wearing something like that? Maybe he had fallen off a boat. Or maybe he was in a play. Or a movie. Maybe they were making a movie, and since I had found him, they would give me a part in the movie.

I liked that idea and had gotten practically to the point of writing the acceptance speech for my Oscar when a movement up the beach caught my eye. Someone was up in the reeds near the Richtors' house. Probably Gary, I thought, and sure enough, when he moved out of the reeds and down onto the sand I could see his greasy black hair and the ever-present cigarette hanging from his lips. Gross, I thought, I hope he doesn't come any closer, and luckily he turned around and headed back up toward his house.

Whew. All I needed was Gary Richtor blowing his disgusting smoke all over me. Gary and his parents had moved in next door to us last winter, and ever since then my main mission in life has been to avoid him. The guy gives me the creeps. Me and practically every other female in Heron's Harbor. In spite of the fact that no woman in her right mind would get anywhere near the guy, he seems to think he's Elvis Presley reincarnated. It's amazing how deluded some people can be. Not that I think Elvis was all that great himself. I never could understand why everyone makes such a big deal about him.

A minute later I heard a siren. That's them, I thought, and I saw Will running down the beach toward me, followed by Mom and the men from the ambulance. When Mom saw the boy she put her hand over her mouth, just as I had. "Oh my. Poor thing," she said.

Then the men were there, moving around him, taking his blood pressure, checking the wound, and loading him onto a stretcher. One of them scribbled some notes on a form and then looked at Mom. "We'll take him right on in to the hospital. We'll need you to come along to fill out a report, since you found him and called in."

"Should my daughter and son come too?" Mom asked. "They actually found him."

"That'll be fine, ma'am. We'll meet you at the emergency room of Franklin General."

They started up the beach carrying the stretcher, and the three of us followed.

We stopped at the house so Mom could get her purse, and then we drove into town to the hospital. One of the men from the ambulance was waiting for us in the emergency room. "Just have a seat over there, ma'am," he told Mom. "The nurse will call you in a minute, and she'll finish up the report."

Mom and I sat down in the only two empty chairs, and Will knelt down on the floor beside a shelf full of magazines and began leafing through them. Across from us sat a woman and a boy. I knew he was her son because they looked a lot alike. They both had curly orange hair, and both could have benefited from a trip to the local Weight Watchers center. The mother was drinking a can of Diet

Coke, and the boy was eating a Milky Way. I wondered why they were there. Was one of them being admitted, or were they visiting someone?

Behind them was a glass wall and through it I saw the boy. He was on one of those rolling carts they use in hospitals, and a nurse was washing the cut on his head. He looked smaller than he had on the beach, and, somehow, more alone. I wondered again who he was and where he had come from.

Then the nurse called Mom, and we moved over to her desk. She asked us some questions about how we had found him, and where, and what time. She made some notes and then had Mom sign some forms.

"I think that's all we need. If you leave your name and phone number, we'll contact you to let you know how he's doing," the nurse said.

"Yes. Thank you. Please let us know," Mom said.

We stood up to leave but I turned back to the nurse. "Do you think it would be okay if I visited him? When he's better, I mean?"

The nurse smiled. "I'm sure he'd like that. I'll check with his doctor and let you know as soon as he's allowed to have visitors."

"Thanks," I said. I don't know why I wanted to see him again, but I did, and somehow I knew that I would.

# 2

"JESSIE. JESSIE, WAKE UP." I heard Will's voice on the edge of my dream. "Jessie . . . come on. You've got to wake up." He shook my shoulder, and this time I did wake up. He stood beside my bed, staring at me with these big solemn eyes, his small face a white circle in the dark room. I pushed myself up on one elbow and looked at the lighted dial of my alarm clock. 2:47.

"Will, what are you doing up? It's the middle of the night." Luckily for him I was still too sleepy and confused to clobber him.

"I know, but I have to talk to you," he said.

I sank back down into my pillow. "Did you have another nightmare? If you're scared you can sleep with me. Get in."

"No. It's not that. I didn't have a nightmare. I just want to talk to you. Come into my room. Please, Jessie. Come on, Jessie, please come." He took my arm, trying to pull me out of bed.

It's funny about this kid. There are times when he makes me so mad that I feel like grabbing the nearest heavy object and smashing him with it, but there are other times when he really gets to me, and I'll do anything he wants me to. For some reason, that night he got to me, so I sat up, yawned, and climbed out of bed. "Okay, I'll come, but you better remember this next time I ask you to do something for me," I told him.

"I will, I promise." He took my hand and led me out of my room and across the hall into his. His room has a big window next to the bed that looks out onto the river. We sat on his bed and looked out at the still, silent night. A pale half-moon was rising, and a golden ribbon of light shone on the black water.

"Look at the moon. It's exactly half-full," I said. It was cold and I pulled his bedspread up over my legs. It was the new bedspread that Mom had just gotten him. It's covered with bright, friendly-looking jungle animals—lions and giraffes and hippos and funny exotic birds. I traced the outline of the lion with my finger.

"Did something scare you?" I asked Will. Lately he had been waking up a lot at night. Once or twice I had heard him crying in the night and had gone into his room to comfort him. Mom's room is down the hall, so I usually hear him first.

But this time Will shook his head. "I was just thinking," he said.

"About the boy?" I asked him.

Will nodded. "And I wondered, what happened to the thing he was holding? The gold thing. Do you know?"

I shook my head. "When I came back to the beach with the blanket, it was gone. I noticed as soon as I went to cover him up. I thought maybe it had just fallen out of his hand, but I looked around on the sand near him. It was gone."

"Where?" Will asked.

I shrugged. "Good question. I wish I knew. It's really weird, isn't it?"

"Do you think we should tell anyone about it?" Will asked.

"I don't know. Actually, I kind of forgot all about it once the men came. And now, I don't know. Let's wait and see."

Will nodded. He crawled up to the head of the bed and got under the covers. Then he hit me with one of his zingers.

"Jessie, do you think I look like Daddy? I mean, do you think I will when I get big?" When he asks me stuff like that I never know what to say. Dad died four years ago, and when Will asks me about him, I'm not sure how to answer him. But I could tell it was important to him, so I said, "Well, you have brown hair like he did. And brown eyes. And you smile kind of like he did. So I guess you do look a little like him."

He didn't say anything for a minute, so I said, "What made you ask that, Will?"

He shrugged. "I don't know. I just wondered." He made his hands into binoculars and put them up to his eyes and peered at me. "I think about him sometimes, and try to remember him, but I can't. I can't remember him."

"You were only two when he died. That's too young to remember, Willy."

"I know . . . but . . . I wish I could remember him. I really wish I could. You're lucky. You were nine when he died."

Did that make me lucky? I wondered. It's true that I remember him. I remember lots of things about him. How tall he was and how big his hands were. The way his cheek felt after he'd shaved, and how he used to bring me Lifesavers sometimes when he came home from work. And how, sometimes, early on a Saturday morning, he would wake me and take me out with him to look at birds. We would walk in the fields or by the shore as the sun came up, and he would point to sparrows and pheasants and gulls and tanagers. And once we saw a marsh hawk circling the fields looking for mice. After our walk we would come home and cook pancakes for Mom and Will, and Mom would always complain about what a mess we made in the kitchen, and Dad would tell her not to worry, we would clean it up later, and then he would wink at me because we both knew that Mom would do it before we got around to it. Am I lucky that I remember all that, or does it just make me sad? I'm not sure, but I do know that sometimes, even now, four years after he died, when I wake up early, I think for a minute that it's one of those Saturdays and that my father is coming to wake me and take me on a bird walk.

"Jessie?"

"What?"

"Do you think Mom and Eric will get married?"

For a minute I didn't say anything. I was surprised actually that he had asked. I hadn't thought he had realized that such a thing was possible. Mom had been going out with Eric for almost a year, and though they hadn't said anything about marriage, I had to admit, they seemed to like each other a lot. And Mom had been acting like a teenager for the last few weeks. She would be in a really rotten mood and then Eric calls, and wham, all of a sudden she's on top of the world and goes around humming sickening tunes like "Love Makes the World Go 'Round" or "I Could Have Danced All Night." Her taste in music is so lame sometimes. But no one had said anything about marriage, and I for one hoped they wouldn't.

It wasn't that I really hated Eric, or anything. And God knows, he was better than some of the other prizes she's dated. Take, for example, Lionel Wallace, or, as Will and I called him, Mr. Fit, the Misfit. He was this health freak she dated a couple of years ago. The whole time she was going out with him there was nothing in our refrigerator but raw carrots and trail mix. He would come over to the house on Saturdays and try to make us all go jogging with him. When that one ended we celebrated by going to McDonald's for dinner and Baskin-Robbin's for dessert.

Then there was the plumber. He wasn't really a plumber. I think he worked in a bank or something, but we called him the plumber because he was always trying to help Mom by tightening pipes and fixing leaky faucets and stuff. Usually all he did was make the faucets worse, and once he even caused a flood in the basement. I think that's when Mom finally stopped seeing him.

Compared to those guys, Eric wasn't bad, but even so, I wasn't happy about the prospect of Mom getting remarried. We were fine the way we were, and we had already had one father. I didn't see any reason why we needed another.

So, anyway, I was surprised that Will had asked about them getting married, and I said, "How should I know, Will? Why don't you ask Mom? It's her life."

I guess I said it in a sharp tone because Will looked kind of hurt, and said, "You don't have to get mad."

"I'm sorry," I told him. "I'm just really tired. I've got to go to sleep, and you do too, okay?"

"Okay. Night, Jessie."

But once I got back to my own room, I couldn't get back to sleep. Like I said, it had been a lousy week, and I had a lot on my mind. I was probably going to flunk science, the first time I've ever come close to flunking anything in my life; I had a crush on Roger Simms, a boy who didn't even know I existed; and my mom had spent the past few weeks acting like a teenager. No wonder I couldn't sleep. Then I thought about the boy we had found. I thought about how he was in the hospital, all alone, and once again I knew for certain that I would be seeing him again. For some reason I felt better, and finally, I fell asleep.

# 3

THE NEXT MONDAY things went from bad to worse. It began with my first close encounter with Roger Simms. First of all, let me give you some selective details about Roger. Picture a blond Matthew Broderick with a Tom Cruise smile. Got it? That's Roger. Of course, as Dana (Dana Andrews, my best friend) said, I didn't know much about his personality. But I figured anyone who looks like that can't be all bad, right? The problem was that whenever I saw him something weird happened to me and I lost all control of my body. Which is what happened on Monday when I was walking backwards out of the science lab, and I ran smack into him. Of course I didn't know it was him until I turned around. When I saw who it was I froze. I mean, like a statue. All I could do was stare at him. I felt the blood rushing around in my body, and I thought, what if I faint right here in front of him, and I couldn't move. I was standing right in the doorway, so no one could go in or out, and I was beginning to create a traffic jam.

Finally Roger said, "Um, excuse me."

I knew I had to say something, but I couldn't get the words to come out of my mouth. I made this weird sort of croaking sound that sounded like I was about to have a heart attack. The traffic jam was getting worse, and finally Dana, who was behind me luckily, sort of shoved me out into the hall, and Roger went on into the science lab.

"Do you realize what a disaster this is?" I said to Dana as soon as I was able to talk again. She was dragging me down the hall toward our homeroom. "Now he thinks I'm a total lunatic."

"No, he doesn't. And anyway, at least he said something to you. I mean, he's noticed you now."

"Yeah, he's noticed me, all right. Next time he sees me he'll run. I mean, the extent of my verbal communications with him consists of a croak. Pretty impressive, huh?"

"Look, Jessie, you've got to get control of this thing. He's just a guy. Just an ordinary guy. One of many who attend Jefferson Jr."

"Ordinary? Have you seen your eye doctor lately? How can you say anyone who looks like that is ordinary? Tommy Klein is ordinary. Jeffrey Burns is ordinary. But Roger Simms is definitely not ordinary."

The bell rang and I realized I was now late for my math class. For the third time in a week. Maybe Dana was right. I had to get control of this thing, whatever this thing was.

When I got to math class I stopped outside the door, took a deep breath, and quietly tiptoed into the room and slid into my seat. Mr. Rabler was writing on the blackboard. He gets very intent when he writes on the blackboard, and doesn't notice much else that's going on in the room, so I thought maybe I was in luck. Maybe he wouldn't even notice that I had been late.

As usual, when Mr. Rabler writes on the blackboard all the kids were doing whatever they felt like doing. Robby Winslow was eating a banana, Marcia Lukins was combing her hair, Freddy Geset had taken off his shoes and socks and was trying to demonstrate the correct way to pick up a pencil with his toes.

As soon as Mr. Rabler put down his chalk and turned around, everyone went back to pretending that they were paying attention. I thought I had it made until he said, "Well, well. So nice of you to grace us with your presence today, Ms. Cameron. Would you mind stopping by my desk after class?"

When class was over I waited until the room had cleared out and then went up to Mr. Rabler's desk. He fixed me with that look of his that always makes me think of a picture from our last year's history text of Napoleon Bonaparte, the short guy from France who won lots of battles. I don't know why he reminds me of that picture, except that his eyes have the same weird way of popping out at you.

Anyway, he stood there staring at me, while I stared at a pile of homework papers on his desk. We stood there like that for a couple of hours—at least it seemed like that to me. Lucky thing I had study hall next. You're allowed to be late to study hall because you're supposed to use the time for teacher conferences. I guess you could call what we were doing a teacher conference, except that so far we hadn't done much conferring. Finally Mr. Rabler got around to saying something. "Well, Ms. Cameron (he pronounced it C*amoron*), it seems you've been having a problem getting to class on time lately. Is this a trend that is likely to continue?"

"No, sir."

"Is there any particular reason why you've been having this problem?"

Now was my chance to come up with something brilliant, like I've been having fainting spells that my doctor says are caused by stress due to academic pressure, or maybe memory lapse that caused me to forget where the math room is . . . but, on second thought, I decided maybe I'd better not try it.

"Umm, no, sir."

"Well then, Ms. Cameron, I suppose my only alternative is to give you a green slip. Please have your parents sign it and return it to Mr. Oglesvy." He filled out a green slip informing my mother that I had been unacceptably late for class three times in a week and handed it to me. He gave me the Napoleon look again, and said, "Let's not have any more of this, all right?"

"Yes, sir—I mean, no, sir."

"Good. You are free to go."

I put the green slip in my backpack along with the note from Mrs. Gibson, the science teacher, telling Mom that I was about to flunk science. Mom was going to have a busy night signing things. I hoped her day was going better than mine. If she was in a bad mood, it was going to be ugly.

I went back to my homeroom and found a note from Mr. Oglesvy on my desk. The note was short and to the point. It said, "Please see me immediately." I didn't know why he wanted to see me, but I was pretty sure it wasn't to congratulate me on the great work I'd been doing lately.

When I got to his office I saw that his door was partially open. He was talking on the phone and motioned for me to wait outside. I sat down on the bench in the hall and waited. In a minute the door opened all the way, and Mr. Oglesvy peered out. He wore his usual expression, which is sort of like a smile, only it's not a real smile. Mr. Oglesvy looks like a cross between Mickey Mouse and John Candy. Really. He's got the weirdest face I've ever seen. He looked at me and said, "Ah, Jessie. Please come in." I stood up and followed him into his office. He sat down behind his desk and motioned for me to sit in the chair across from him. There was an open file on his desk and he studied it for a minute. Then he looked up at me, cocked his head to one side, and said, "You know, Jessie, I'm disturbed. I'm very disturbed."

I didn't know what to say. Did he want my condolences or what? I decided that saying nothing was the best

policy. I looked at the floor. I noticed that the rug was probably one of the ugliest rugs I had ever seen in my life. No wonder he's disturbed, I thought. I'd be disturbed, too, if I had to look at that rug every day. It was purple with little squiggles of gold running through it, like little worms.

"Do you know why I'm disturbed, Jessie?"

I could have guessed the rug, but I thought I'd be better off sticking to my policy of silence, so I just shook my head.

"I'm disturbed because I spoke with your science teacher this morning, and she informs me that you are close to failing. I've also heard from other teachers that you are not handing in your homework and that you are coming to class late." He folded his hands and rested them on top of the file on his desk. Then he leaned forward, staring at me.

I stared at the rug.

"Can you explain this, Jessie?"

I shook my head. On the shelf behind his desk was a picture of his family. I had seen them at school. Sometimes they came to sports events and school plays. The little boy had the biggest ears of any kid I had ever seen. He looked a lot like his father. He had the same Mickey Mouse nose.

"I wonder, Jessie, do you see any kind of a pattern developing here?"

A pattern? Was he talking about the rug now? I continued to stare at it, trying to look as if I was uncovering a pattern.

He shuffled some papers on his desk and then cleared his throat. "In the past your work has been consistently above average, Jessie. Not quite honor role standards, but nevertheless above average. And most of your teachers seem to feel you have the ability to do even better if you would apply yourself. In the last month, however, your work has slipped noticeably. I might even say drastically. Do you have any idea why?"

Something in his voice made me look up. He had sounded as if he really wanted to know the answer. And when I looked at him, I saw that he looked . . . puzzled and, well, concerned. And I thought, maybe he actually cares. Maybe he really wants to understand. And for a minute I really wanted him to understand. The only problem was, I didn't understand it myself.

"It's only science that's a real problem," I said. After all, it wasn't as if other kids didn't flunk things occasionally. Why did he have to pick on me?

"Well, science is the worst case, certainly, but your other grades are slipping as well. And it's not only the grades, Jessie, it's your attitude. You know, we take pride in our students here at Jefferson Jr., and we expect our students to take pride in themselves. That means being on time for classes, handing assignments in on time, doing your best work, and showing respect for your teachers."

"Yes, sir," I said, trying to put respect in my voice. But all I could think of was the Aretha Franklin song, RESPECT. My mother has a tape called "Soul Hits of the Sixties," and that's one of her favorites.

I had been hoping that the interview was almost at an end, but I should have known better. Oglesvy is renowned for his ability to talk endlessly about nothing. He leaned back in his chair, getting comfortable. "You see, Jessie, I have a theory. My theory goes like this. When students take pride in themselves, that pride is reflected in the school. The school looks good. It feels good. It does what it's supposed to do, which is, of course, to educate young people. It's the same with people, Jessie. When a person takes pride in himself, or herself, you can tell. He looks and feels good. He does his job. You know, when I interview a prospective student, or a prospective employee, I always look at their shoes. Do you know why?"

"No, sir," I said carefully. I wondered if this was some kind of trick to see if I was paying attention. I was confused. A minute before we had been talking about education. Now we were talking about shoes.

"Shoes say a lot about a person, Jessie. When a person's shoes are polished and well kept, that's a clue. A clue that that person takes pride in himself."

I looked at my battered running shoes. I wondered what kind of clues they gave him. I tried to look under the desk to see what his shoes looked like. Polished wing tips, I was sure. He was quiet for a minute and I figured he was running out of steam.

"Well, I'd better get to class, Mr. Oglesvy. I don't want to get behind."

He jumped up so suddenly from his chair that I thought for a minute he was angry. But he beamed at me and said, "That's the spirit, my girl. I'm glad we understand each other."

"Yes, sir."

"Well, then, I'll expect to see some improvement in those grades by the end of the semester."

I nodded as he opened the door, and I escaped into the empty hallway. The late bell was just about to ring, but I made it to history just in time. I sat down, took out my book, and looked over at Dana.

"Where were you?" she whispered.

"Oglesvy's office."

"Why?"

"He gave me a lecture because my grades are slipping. The man is even weirder than I thought. I think he's got a shoe fetish."

"He should get together with Freddy." She nodded at Freddy, who was taking off his shoes and socks again.

Anyway, you get the picture. My life was not getting any easier, and I had this weird feeling that things were going to get worse before they got better.

# 4

YOU DON'T HAVE TO BE A GENIUS to know when my
mother is in one of her moods. The signs are pretty clear.
When she's in a bad mood, the first thing she does when she
comes home from work is to go straight to the refrigerator.
She yanks it open and then stands there in front of it staring
and shaking her head. It's like some horrible, unspeakable
act is taking place in there. Then she slams the refrigerator
door and calls out for a pizza. Whenever we have pizza for
dinner you know my mother is in a bad mood.

And when my mother is in a bad mood, the best thing
to do is keep quiet and stay out of her way. It is definitely
not the time to let her in on what's been going on in school
lately, unless you made honor roll or were elected presi-
dent of student council.

So, when my mother came home that night and began
her refrigerator routine, I decided that it was not the night to
get her to sign the green slip and the note from Mrs. Gibson.

I decided I would just tell Mr. Oglesvy that she was out of town and therefore couldn't sign anything. This may sound like a lie to you, but actually it's not, because our house is outside of the town limits, so technically, when my mother's home she's out of town. See? I may be a lot of things but I'm no liar.

I left my mother staring into the refrigerator and went into the den. Will was sitting on the floor rooting through my backpack.

"What do you think you're doing?" I said, grabbing it away from him.

"Nothing. I was just looking for your Gameboy."

"Well, it's not in there, and I wouldn't let you use it anyway. Last time I lent it to you you got bubble gum stuck all over it."

"What's this green piece of paper say? Aren't you sup-posed to get Mom to sign it?"

I spun around to look at him. He was still sitting on the floor, arms crossed, and there was a smirk on his face that told me he knew he had me right where he wanted me. I considered my options. Should I bribe him or threaten him?

"Well, you *are* going to tell her, aren't you? She has to sign it, right?"

"I'm aware of that, Dorkface, and I'll tell her in my own good time, and if you dare open your mouth about this I'll chop you up into little tiny pieces and feed you to your goldfish. And I'd probably receive a medal for doing it."

"Just let me play with your Gameboy and I promise I won't tell."

I took the Gameboy out of my pocket and tossed it to him. "If you get bubble gum on it, it'll be the last time you ever play with it."

"I won't. I promise."

"And if you ever go through my backpack again you'll be sorry."

I stomped out of the den and back into the kitchen. Mom slammed the refrigerator door and said, "Call Pizzatown. Get the works."

"No pepperoni," Will shouted from the den.

He hates pepperoni and I love it. I ordered half with pepperoni and half without.

So then I guess Mom decided that she should act like a real mother, and she says, "So tell me what happened in school today."

"Nothing," I say.

"Nothing? You mean you spent eight hours there and nothing happened? Absolutely nothing?"

I hate it when she does this. "Nothing special," I say. "I mean, I went to class, I went to lunch, I went to more classes. I came home. It was a thrilling day, like always."

Then all of a sudden she drops the laundry basket she's holding and the clothes spill all over the floor. Then she takes hold of my shoulders and says, "Why don't you ever talk to me anymore? You used to tell me everything. Now I can't get anything out of you."

"I'm talking to you now, Mom," I say. "See, my lips are moving. Words are coming out of my mouth. See?"

"But you know what I mean. I feel like you never really tell me anything."

I have to admit, I felt a little guilty then, because of the green slip and all, and I thought, maybe this is the time to tell her, but then the phone rings and it's Eric of course. My mom rushes to the phone and when she finds out it's him she gets all excited. "Just a minute," she tells him. "Jessie, I'm going upstairs. Hang this up when I get on the other phone, okay, sweetie? And say hello." She hands me the receiver and dashes upstairs.

"Hi, Eric," I say.

"Jess. How are you?"

"Fine."

"Good. Okay, how'd the math test go?"

"Okay, I guess. He hasn't handed them back yet, so I don't know what I got."

"Okay, Jess. You can hang up now," Mom says.

I hung up and decided I'd better start looking for money for the pizza man, because I knew Mom would still be on the phone when he came. I could guarantee it.

A few nights earlier Eric had been over and I'd been stuck on some algebra problems that I needed to understand for a test the next day, and Mom had asked him to help me with them. He explained it pretty well, I have to admit.

Will and I had started eating the pizza when Mom finally came downstairs. You would have thought she was a different woman. No more refrigerator staring. No more sighing. And she was humming again. One of those show tunes from some fifties movie.

Eric is a psychologist. It really drives me crazy the way he always seems to be prying into my life. Like the way he's always asking me how I feel about things. I say, "I got a D on my science test." He says, "How do you feel about that?" I say, "It's raining out." He says, "How do you feel about that?" I say, "I broke my leg and I'm dying of tuberculosis." He says, "How do you feel about that?" It's kind of a dumb question if you ask me. Anyway, I always say, "I don't know," and then he looks all sad and disappointed, like he was waiting for some deep revelation.

I have to admit, though, he tries hard to be nice. But it's pretty obvious that he's only trying because he likes Mom. He even tries to bribe us by bringing us things. Last time he came back from a trip he brought Will *The Pop-Up Book of Baseball* and me a pair of earrings shaped like cats. The bribes are working well with Will. He thinks Eric is terrific.

"So how's Eric, Mom?" I asked.

"Oh, he's fine. Just great. He's coming for dinner tomorrow. He's going to stop at Zaburn's and pick up barbecued ribs, so all I have to do is make a salad and get some rolls."

"Can he take me to the game next week?" Will asked.

"I don't know, sweetie," Mom said happily. She brushed hair out of his eyes. "You'll have to ask him. I'm sure he'd love to if he's not busy."

The whole scene was beginning to make me a little ill. I finished my second piece of pizza, and said, "Well, I've got homework. I'm gonna go get started."

A few minutes later the phone rang again. Mom answered it, and I heard her talking. When she hung up she called up to me, "Jess, that was the hospital calling about the boy."

I went to the top of the stairs. "How is he?" I asked.

"Well, he's better. They said he's in stable condition, and they expect a full recovery."

"Have they found his parents?" I asked.

"Apparently not," she said. "It's very odd, isn't it? They said he's sustained a temporary memory loss, so they're having trouble locating his family."

"A memory loss? You mean like amnesia?" I asked.

"I guess so. She said it's not uncommon in head injuries. She seemed to think it would only be temporary."

"Amnesia. Weird. Is he allowed to have visitors?" I asked.

"Yes. The nurse seemed to think it would do him good. Would you like to go see him after school tomorrow? You could just walk over and then catch the late bus home."

"Okay," I said.

"Can I go too?" Will asked.

"I think Jessie'd better go alone tomorrow. Maybe you can go next time," Mom told him.

I went back to my room and tried to work on my homework, but I couldn't stop thinking about the boy. What would he be like? I tried to imagine, but I couldn't. Tomorrow, I thought. Tomorrow I'll see him again.

# 5

THE NEXT DAY, as soon as school was out, I walked the
five blocks from school to the hospital. I've never been in
the hospital to stay, and I had visited it only twice before,
once when Will was born, and once when my grandmother
had an operation.

I was seven when Will was born, and I came with Dad
to see Mom and the new baby. I remember holding Dad's
hand as we went up in the elevator and down the hall, and
standing with him, peering through the glass partition at
all the newborn babies. Dad asked me to guess which one
Will was, but I guessed the wrong one. And then he pointed
to this scrawny, red-faced little baby with a solemn expression and said, "There he is. That's him."

I didn't want to say anything to Dad, because it was
pretty obvious that he thought Will was terrific, but I
thought he was just about the ugliest baby I'd ever seen. I
kept watching him, though, the way his little face worked,

and the way he looked around so seriously, as if he was trying to understand what was happening to him, and after a while I kind of got to like him. By the end of the visit, I thought that Will was definitely the best baby there.

That had been six years ago, but the hospital looked and smelled exactly the same; it had the antiseptic smell that reminds me of the nurse's office at school.

When I got to the hospital I went to the admitting desk and said to the clerk, "I'm Jessie Cameron. I'm here to visit the boy that we found on the beach last Friday. I don't know his name, but one of the nurses called last night and said he was better and it would be okay if I came to see him."

"You must mean John Thomas in 305. He came in on the twenty-ninth with a concussion, right?"

"Well, he had a bad cut on his head."

"Yes, that's him. He's in room 305. Through the gray doors and left to the elevators. The floor nurse can tell you where his room is."

"Thanks."

I followed her directions up to the third floor and asked at the nurses' station for room 305. A young nurse said, "Oh, you're here to see John? You must be Jessie Cameron. He's eager to meet you. Just follow me and I'll show you to his room."

I was nervous as I followed her down the hall. What would he be like, I wondered. Would I like him? Would he like me?

The door was partway open, and the nurse knocked and said, "You have a visitor, John."

He said, "Come in," and nurse stood aside to let me go in. "Not too long," she told me. "We don't want to tire him. So please stay only a few minutes."

He was sitting up in bed holding the remote control for the television that was hanging from the ceiling in one corner of the room. It was a small room, just big enough for the bed, one chair, and a little sink. His head was wrapped in a white bandage, and he wore a blue hospital gown. He looked a lot better than he had looked the last time I had seen him. I walked over to the bed. "Hi. I'm Jessie Cameron," I said.

He held out his hand and I shook it. "John Thomas," he said.

"How are you feeling?" I asked him. I didn't know what else to say.

"A lot better, thank you. Yesterday my head hurt horribly, but today it feels better."

"That's good. It was an awful-looking cut. It was . . . . " I was about to tell him how it was all swollen and purple, but then I thought maybe I'd better not go into that. "It looked pretty painful."

"Yes, I guess I banged it up pretty bad." He paused and then said, "Listen, I want to thank you. For . . . for finding me and all."

I shrugged. "I didn't do anything. All we did was call the ambulance. And actually it was my little brother who really found you. He was playing down the beach and all of a sudden he came running. I went up to see what he'd found and there you were, just lying there. I . . . I thought at first you might have been . . . . "

"Dead?"

"Well, yeah. I was so relieved when I felt a pulse and I knew you were alive."

He pointed to the chair. "Do you want to sit down? They probably won't let you stay long, but someone might as well use the chair."

"Umm, have they been able to contact your family yet?"

He shook his head. He didn't seem to want to talk about that, so I changed the subject.

"Have they told you how long you'll be in here?"

"No. They haven't said."

I pulled the chair over closer to the bed and sat down. I was dying to ask him what he had been doing on the beach, and where his family was, and why no one had been looking for him, but I was afraid I might upset him. I tried to think of something else to talk about.

"How's the food?" I asked finally. Kind of a lame topic of conversation, I know, but I didn't know what else to say.

"Not too bad."

"I've never been in the hospital. I mean, not to stay. Just to visit."

"Me either," he said, "until now."

I was just about to ask him if the nurses were nice when he said, "Umm. I wondered, did you happen to find a watch anywhere around the spot where you found me? I'm missing my watch, and it's most awfully important that I find it."

"Was it a pocket watch?" I asked. "A round gold pocket watch with a chain?"

He sat up quickly. "Yes. Yes, that's it. Did you find it?"

He sounded so happy that I hated to tell him the truth. "No. We saw it. You were holding it when we first found you. It was in your hand. We left you to call the ambulance, and when I came back down, it was gone. I looked around the beach, but it wasn't there. It was so strange. It just vanished."

"I . . . I don't understand. You mean I had it? I had it in my hand, and then it was gone?"

I nodded. "I know it sounds strange, but. . ."

"But it must be on the beach. I must have dropped it or something," he said.

I shook my head, "I've looked. I've been back a few times since to look again. It's gone."

"No," he cried. He lay back with a sigh and for a minute I was afraid he was going to cry. "I have to find it . . . It's terribly important. You don't understand how important it is. What could have happened to it?"

I shrugged. I wondered why it was so important. It seemed to me he had a few other things to worry about besides a watch. Like where his family was, and why he couldn't remember anything. But he kept on obsessing about this watch.

"Someone must have taken it," I said. "There's no other explanation."

"Who?" he asked. He stared at me, and for a minute he looked a little desperate, but then he seemed to pull himself together. "I'm sorry. It's not your problem. Tell me about your brother. How old is he?"

"He's six," I told him, glad that we had moved on from the watch. "He can be a pain sometimes, but mostly he's okay. That day he found you, I knew something had really scared him. He gets scared a lot, but this was different. He'd been up the beach playing Ninja Turtles, and all of a sudden he came charging."

"Playing what?" he asked.

"Ninja Turtles. You know, heroes on the half shell, turtle power. Raphael and Michelangelo?"

He still looked blank.

"Don't tell me you've never heard of the Ninja Turtles?"

"Oh, yes. I guess I just forgot." he said.

Then I remembered about the amnesia and I felt really stupid. "Yeah. I'm sorry." I wanted to ask what it was like, not being able to remember anything, but I didn't want to upset him.

Then the door opened and the nurse stuck her head in. "Sorry, guys, but I'm afraid your time is up." She came into the room with her thermometer and stuck it in his mouth. "We can't let him get tired, you know. He's just beginning to mend."

"Sure, I understand," I said, and, to tell you the truth, I was kind of relieved. It was hard thinking of things to talk about that wouldn't upset him. I stood up to go, and he held up his hand, motioning for me to wait until the nurse took the thermometer out of his mouth.

"Hmmm. Only 100.6. You're getting better. Maybe your visitor did you some good. But let's not overdo it."

"Will you come back?" he asked me.

"Sure, I can come after school again. And I'll bring Will. He's dying to meet you, but Mom said not today."

"Thank you for coming," he said as I followed the nurse out the door.

As we walked down the hall the nurse said, "I really think you helped him. Poor thing. It's awfully lonely for him. If only we'd hear from his family. I just can't understand it. Someone must be looking for him. And he can't seem to remember a thing except his name. The amnesia's temporary, I'm certain, but it's awfully hard for now." When we reached the elevator, she said, "Well, here we are. Do come back tomorrow. It's sure to help."

"I will," I told her.

Outside the hospital the sun was going down, and it was getting colder. As I walked back to school to catch the late bus home, I thought about the boy. Why hadn't anyone come for him? Where were his parents, his family? Didn't anyone care about him? It didn't make any sense. He wasn't the kind of person that no one cares about. It was all so weird. I had to find out more about him. I knew I wouldn't be able to stop thinking about him until I did.

# 6

"DON'T YOU HAVE ANY PARENTS?" Will asked. He stood by the boy's hospital bed, looking at him with his solemn expression. I had known he might ask something like that, but I hadn't thought it would be the first thing out of his mouth. Not that I wasn't dying to know the answer myself, but still, we had been there approximately thirty seconds. I mean, he could have waited.

"I have parents," said the boy, "but it's impossible for them to come right now."

"Oh. Don't you miss them?" asked Will. He had wandered over to the sink and was looking at himself in the mirror. "You have your own sink. Cool."

"Will," I said, "that's not exactly any of your business."

"That's all right," said the boy. "Yes, I do miss them, actually."

"So you've gotten your memory back?" I asked. Maybe I shouldn't have, but it just kind of slipped out. I mean, if he remembered his parents he couldn't have amnesia any-more, right?

He looked at me for a minute as if trying to decide what to say. "Actually," he said, "I never really lost my memory. I just let them think that to avoid questions."

"Huh? You never had amnesia?" I said. One of us was definitely confused, and at that point I wasn't sure whether it was him or me.

He shook his head. "I remember everything perfectly. And, by the way, my name isn't John Thomas. I just made that up. I couldn't decide between John or Tom, so I chose John Thomas. My real name is Reuben. Reuben Miller."

I stared at him. Wait a minute, I thought, this was getting too weird. He had never had amnesia? He had made it all up, including his name?

"But . . . why? Why did you tell them you had am-nesia? Why did you give them a false name? And, and why . . . " I stopped, even though there were a million more questions I wanted to ask.

He seemed to know what I was thinking. "Why haven't I contacted my family? Why haven't I told anyone where I come from? Why hasn't anyone been to see me? Except for you two, of course. It must seem very odd."

"Well, yes." Odd wasn't the word for it. I'd call it downright bizarre.

"But not half as odd as the truth," he said.

If this had been an episode of "The Twilight Zone" they would have started playing that creepy music right about now—doodoo doodoo doodoo doodoo. But this wasn't a TV show, so what was going on?

"What do you mean?" I asked him.

He sighed and lay back against his pillows. "Just what I said. If I told you the truth you wouldn't believe me. No one would. It's . . . too hard to believe."

"Try me," I said. I didn't know if I'd believe him or not, but whatever he was going to tell me, I wanted to hear it. I was so curious I *had* to hear it.

He looked at me for a long time, and I could tell this was no joke. I began to feel a little scared. What was this thing he was going to tell us? Finally he said, "Do you really want to know?"

I nodded.

"You won't believe me," he said with a sigh. "It's too impossible. I can hardly believe it myself. You'll think I'm mad. You'll think the bump on my head did more damage than they thought. I thought that myself at one point. I thought this was all just a hallucination, or a dream . . ." He shook his head. "It's just too hard to believe."

"Are you in some kind of trouble?" I asked him. Kind of a stupid question, but . . . what could it be—this secret that was so impossible to believe?

"Not the kind you're thinking of," he said.

He was sitting up in bed again, and his head was still bandaged, but there was color in his face. He looked healthier than he had looked the day before. And he didn't look crazy.

"I think I'm going to tell you. I've got to tell someone, and . . . I need your help. I . . . I don't know what to do."

"Well, go ahead. We're listening."

"Can he keep a secret?" Reuben asked, glancing at Will who was playing with the remote control for the TV.

I nodded. That was one thing about Will. He was kind of a quiet kid, and he didn't tell things. I know other little kids who tell everyone everything, but Will was different. "He's good that way. Not like most kids," I told him.

Reuben took a deep breath and said, "Well, all right." Then he stopped and smiled. "It's kind of hard to know where to start," he said.

"Start at the beginning," I said. Easy to say. It's not always that simple. I know that now.

"I guess I should start with the watch. You saw it, right? You saw it in my hand."

I nodded.

"It's . . . It's not an ordinary watch. It's very . . . special," said Reuben.

"Is it magic?" asked Will.

"Don't be silly, Will," I said. "You know there's no such thing as magic."

But Reuben looked at Will and said, "Let's just say it's a very unusual watch. As for magic, well, I guess there are lots of different kinds of magic. Sometimes what people think is magic is just something they don't understand."

"So tell us about the watch. Why is it so special?" I was trying to sound cool and calm, but I didn't feel it. I wasn't

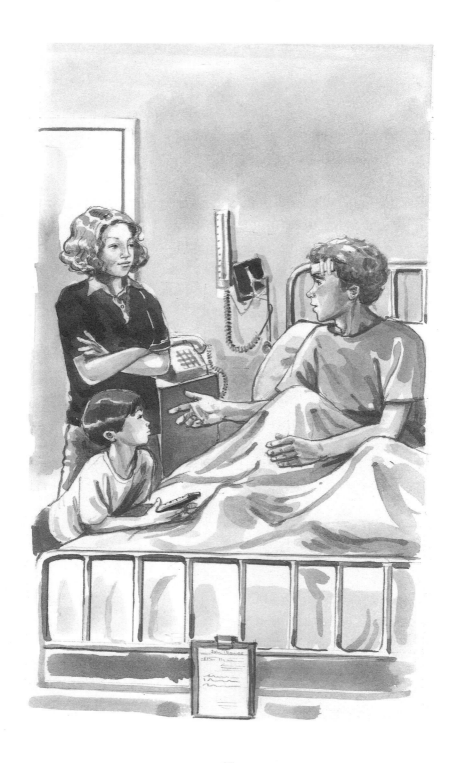

sure if he was crazy or lying or what. All I knew was that it was too late now. I had to hear what he was going to say.

"It was my grandfather's. He gave it to me four years ago, when I was ten. That was just three months before he died."

"Oh, well, no wonder it's special to you," I said. I was kind of relieved. This was an explanation I could deal with.

"Well, yes. But that's not the only reason," said Reuben.

"What do you mean?" I asked.

Reuben didn't answer for a minute. Then he said, "As I said, it's a long story. Are you sure you want to hear it?"

Uh-oh. Here we go again. "Yes. Tell us. Please."

"First let me tell you something about my grandfather. See, he was a scientist. A physicist, actually. He spent years studying light waves, and trying to understand how they travel through space. He invented lots of things, special lenses for telescopes and cameras, and lots of other things."

"Was he famous?" asked Will.

"Well, you've probably never heard of him, but other scientists knew of his work. Anyway, about ten years before he died, he became interested in time, and how time and motion affect the movement of light. He worked with a friend of his, a clockmaker named Mr. Vonstrook. They had been working together for several years when they got involved in a secret project. They started working all the time, but they wouldn't tell anyone what the project was all about.

"Then one day my grandfather's housekeeper sent a message to my mother to tell her that she was worried about my grandfather. She said that he and Mr. Vonstrook had been locked up in his laboratory, and they hadn't come out for two days."

Reuben stopped talking for a minute and I wondered what all this had to do with why he was here, and where he had come from. I mean, sure, it was an interesting story, and I'm sure his grandfather was a very nice man and all, but I didn't understand what this had to do with anything. Then he went on with the story.

"My parents had a key to the laboratory, and they went to check on him. They knocked and knocked, but no one answered, so finally they went inside. They found that the laboratory was empty, although the housekeeper swears my grandfather never left. My parents decided that he and Mr. Vonstrook had gone away on a trip that had something to do with this secret project they were working on. He was away for two weeks, and when he returned he wouldn't tell anyone where he had been."

"Did you ever find out where he had been?" I asked.

Reuben shook his head. "He never told anyone. Soon after they returned, his friend Mr. Vonstrook became sick and died. Shortly after his death, my grandfather retired and closed up his laboratory. He spent all his time reading and writing stories, mostly science fiction stories.

"About a year before he died he got sick and was confined to bed. I used to go over to his house most afternoons on my way home from school, and we'd talk about all kinds of things."

As he talked, Reuben stared out the window. It seemed as if he had almost forgotten that Will and I were there.

"It was on my tenth birthday that he gave me the watch. I'll never forget what he said that day. He asked me if I had ever had the experience of looking for something, and finding that it was right in front of my eyes all along. I told him that I had and he said, 'Well, when you are searching for answers, you will find the same thing is true. Until you are ready to see the truth, it will be hidden from you.' Then he told me he had a present for me, and he gave me the watch. I had never seen it before, but as soon as I saw it I knew that it was a very special watch. With the watch was a small package. The package was wrapped up in brown paper and tied with string. When he handed it to me he said, 'You're a good boy, and you're the one I've chosen to entrust with these. They are the products of my life's work. They are for you alone. Use them wisely.' Then he told me that I must not open the package until after his death."

"You couldn't open the present?" asked Will.

"Weren't you curious?" I asked.

"Curious? I was beyond curious. I was obsessed by that package. I imagined all kinds of things inside it. I spent hours in my room just staring at it, trying to imagine what was in it. My parents even noticed that I was acting strange. During the last weeks of his life my grandfather was in a coma. I would go to see him and read to him, but he never woke up. I knew he was going to die, and that made me sad, but I knew that when he died I could open the package. That last week seemed to take forever.

"Finally one night we got a message that he had died. I wanted to run to my closet right then and rip open the package, but that would have seemed so . . . I don't know, like a vulture or something, waiting for him to die. I made myself wait until after his funeral. Then I took the package and went out into the woods behind our house, to a special hiding place I had there, and I opened it."

"And? What was it?" I asked.

"It was a book. A book of stories that he had written. They were good stories, but still, I found it hard to believe that this was all. This was what I had been so curious about, so obsessed with, for the past months. Just a few stories."

"What kind of stories were they?" I asked.

"They were science fiction. There were about two men who invented a watch that could transport them to other times. The two men travel together through time, and the stories recount their travels. All except for the last one. In that story, the men show a group of scientists what they've found. The scientists all start making their own time traveling instruments, and pretty soon they start selling them to the public. Everyone begins traveling around through time, and the world becomes more and more chaotic until finally, at the end of that story time stops, and the world is frozen in time. It's kind of an eerie story."

Yeah, I guess so, I thought. "So what did you do with them?" I asked.

"Nothing. I just put them in my drawer. I didn't even show anyone, because I didn't think my grandfather had wanted me to. Gradually I thought about them less and less. I had almost forgotten they existed until just a few days ago when I realized something."

"What do you mean?" I asked.

"They weren't made-up stories. Except for the last one, all of those stories were true. They really happened."

I didn't say anything. I just sat there looking at him. The stories were true, he said. His grandfather's stories about people traveling through time were true? That meant . . . doodoo doodoo doodoo doodoo.

# 7

I STARED. I GAWKED. I looked at him as if he were nuts. Was he actually saying what I thought he was saying?

"Wait a minute," I said, shaking my head. "I . . . I don't think I understand. What do you mean the stories were true? Which stories?"

"My grandfather's stories. They were all true. All except the last one."

"I don't get it."

He sighed and then spoke very slowly, as if he were talking to a little kid. "The stories, they weren't actually stories, they were a diary. Those things actually happened. He and Mr. Vonstrook, they learned how to travel through time."

"Wait a minute. Wait wait wait wait wait. Let me get this straight. You're saying that your grandfather actually traveled through time like . . . like Michael J. Fox? Come on, Reuben. It's impossible."

He had been right. It was too hard to believe. I was thinking all the things he had said I would think, like his injury had been worse than they thought. It wasn't just amnesia that he had, it was worse. The kid was a lunatic. A raving lunatic. The only question was, had he always been this way, or had the bump on his head caused it?

"You think I'm mad, don't you?" he asked. "I don't blame you. I would have thought the same thing if I were you. In fact I thought I was mad for a while. But then I remembered some things my grandfather said, and suddenly it all made sense, as unbelievable as it seemed. And of course, it happened to me. I can't dispute that."

"What do you mean, it happened to you? What are you saying?"

"Jessie, the day you found me on the beach, what was the date, do you remember?"

"Well, it was five days ago, and today's October 3rd, so it would have been September, umm 29th. Why?"

"So it was September 29, 1992, right?"

"Right."

"Well, the last thing I remember was being on my uncle's oyster boat. I was helping him out for a weekend. That night a storm blew up, and I was up on deck."

"Yeah, so?"

"Well, you know what the date was that day?"

Uh-oh, I thought. Here we go again. I wasn't sure I even wanted to hear what he was going to say this time.

"I give up. What was the date?" I asked.

"It was September 29th, 1892. I was knocked out in the storm, and I woke up one hundred years later. I know it sounds strange. I know it's hard to believe. When I woke up here in this hospital, I . . . I thought I was dreaming. That thing, that television . . . I thought . . . I didn't know what it was! I was so scared I started screaming. They gave me an injection and I went back to sleep, but when I woke up again, nothing had changed. The dream was still the same. Or the nightmare, I should say. Then I remembered that in one of my grandfather's stories he talked about a box with moving pictures. They called it a television. In the story he goes into how it works. I didn't understand it, but I see now. And this." He pointed to the phone on the stand by his bed. "A telephone. I've read about the telephone, and one of my friends saw one when he went to Baltimore, but I didn't think they looked like this."

"You don't have a television?" Will asked.

"No. No, it hasn't been invented yet. I . . . there are so many things I haven't seen. So much I don't understand. You can see why I need your help." He looked at me, and for a minute he looked really scared and, well, desperate. "Do you . . . do you believe me?"

I didn't say anything. Actually, I couldn't say anything. The room was doing weird things all of a sudden, and I felt as if my head was spinning. The air felt clammy and for a minute I was afraid I was going to faint. Maybe I'm dreaming, I thought. I looked at Will. He was leaning on the bottom of the bed, looking at Reuben with what Mom calls his Professor Stein expression. She calls it his Professor Stein expression because it reminds her of a professor she had in college who looked like that whenever he was trying to answer a question. He kind of pulls his eyebrows together and sticks his lips out. I reached out and pulled him over to me. I thought maybe if I held onto him it would make me feel better. He squirmed away from me, though, and went back to the end of the bed. I stood up and went to the sink to get a glass of water. I could see Reuben in the mirror, and our eyes met. The scared look was gone, and now he looked only resigned.

"I knew you wouldn't believe me," he said. "I shouldn't have told you. Now you think I'm mad."

"Noooo. I wouldn't say that, exactly," I said, although I was lying, and we all knew it. "It's just . . . "

"Yes, I know. Wait a minute," he said. He reached over to the drawer in the table beside his bed and pulled out a small leather sack. He untied the drawstring and shook out some coins. "Look at these," he said, holding them out for me and Will to see.

I took the coins from him and looked them over. At first they looked like plain old pennies and dimes and nickels. But then I noticed there were some differences, so I checked the dates. All of them were from 1890 or before. Why would he have all these coins from back then? Well, I thought, he could be a coin collector. Now if you ask me, collecting coins is weird, but it's a lot less weird than falling off a boat and waking up on a beach a hundred years later.

I shrugged. "You could be a collector," I said.

"I could be, but I'm not. That's my life's savings," he said.

"That's all the money you have? I've got almost three dollars," Will said.

"Yeah, but this was worth a lot more back then, Will," I told him. "You know, inflation? That thing Mom always complains about at the grocery store?"

"Oh. Well, anyway, my money's not with me. It's at home in my guard dog."

"In your what?" Reuben asked.

"His guard dog. It's a stuffed dog with a little safe in it. If anyone tries to steal anything from the safe, the dog barks. It works on a battery," I explained. "So don't ever try to steal anything from Will. No point in trying for a loan either. You'd have more chance getting money out of Scrooge McDuck. I speak from experience."

"Jessie never has money. She always tries to borrow," Will said.

I handed the coins back to Reuben. "Well, I guess we better be going. We don't want to miss the bus, Willy," I said. All of a sudden I wanted to go. I had to think about this, and I couldn't think in that stuffy hospital room.

Reuben sighed. "I guess you won't be coming back," he said.

"Yes, we will," Will told him. "I believe you. About being from a hundred years ago. You don't sound like a boy from now."

I had to admit, the kid was right. Reuben did have sort of an accent, and the way he phrased things . . . but still.

"Thank you, Will. That means a lot to me," Reuben told him.

"Don't get too excited. I mean, he's only six; his concept of time is still a little hazy. He just figured out that there are twelve months in a year." And hey, I thought, he still believes in the Easter Bunny and the Tooth Fairy. Why not a boy who can travel through time?

"Jessie, I believe him," Will said.

"Okay, okay. So you believe him. That doesn't mean I have to," I said. "I mean, explain to me, please, just how it happened? And why you? And why here? It just doesn't make sense."

"It's the watch, don't you see?" Reuben said. "That's why I'm so worried about getting it back. Without that watch I . . . I'll never get home."

"You'll be stuck here, a century away from home," I said. And then it hit me, just how bad his situation really was. If he was telling the truth, if somehow he had really flown through time, he had a big problem. A *big* problem.

"But why the watch?" I asked. "I mean, how does it work?"

"The watch is what my grandfather and Mr. Vonstrook were working on for all those years. Actually, two watches. According to my grandfather's stories, they both had one. I don't understand exactly how it works, though my grandfather goes into some of the principles in his writing. It's very complicated and involves the theory of relativity and a whole lot of other scientific formulas. The one thing I do remember, though, is that in the stories, the catalyst that made the watch work was simultaneous contact with both fire and water."

"You mean it has to be touching water and fire at the same time?" I asked.

Reuben nodded. "Right. And see, the way it works in the stories is that you set the calendar for whatever date you want to go to, and then activate it by touching it with fire and water in the same instant."

I watched him as he spoke. He wasn't lying. He believed what he was telling me. There were only two possibilities: either he was crazy, or it was all true.

"So what happened? Did you activate the watch on purpose, or what?" I asked him.

"I've been thinking about that constantly since I woke up in this hospital bed, and what I think happened is this. See, I was sitting on deck watching the storm blow in right before it happened. I remember taking my watch out of my pocket and I noticed that it had stopped so I started to wind it. I was holding it in my hand when the storm really blew up. A gust of wind caused the boat to heel almost over, and a huge wave hit us. The last thing I remember is an incredibly intense flash of light. Lightning, I guess."

"So the watch activated because of the wave and the lightning hitting it at the same time?" I asked.

"I think that's what must have happened. When I first woke up here in the hospital, I thought I must have been struck by lightning, but there were no signs—no burns or anything. But the lightning must have struck the watch, or close enough to it to activate it. And I must have set it to the wrong date by mistake. 1992 instead of 1892."

"Guess you'll be more careful next time you set your watch, huh?" I said.

"So anyway, here I am. It took me a long time to work it all out, what had happened, I mean. And at first I couldn't believe it either. But I remembered my grandfather's stories, and, of course, I couldn't deny the evidence."

Could it be true? I didn't know what to believe. There was something about him that made me want to trust him, to believe him, but . . .

There was a knock on the door and the nurse stuck her head into the room. "John, the doctor will be here in just a minute to change your dressing and take a look at you. I think your friends had better go now."

"Okay." I was relieved, ready to get out of there.

When the nurse had gone, Reuben said, "I know you probably don't believe me. I don't blame you. I'd like it if you'd come back, but I'll understand if you don't."

"I'll come back," said Will.

I didn't say anything. I didn't know yet if I would come back or not.

"Would you do one thing for me, though?" he said.

"If I can," I said.

"Would you call me? On the telephone? I've never gotten a telephone call before, and I just want to try it."

I was relieved. A phone call was easy. "Sure. No problem. Let me just write down the number and I'll call you tonight." I jotted his number on the cover of my notebook. "Life without a phone," I shuddered. "It must be horrible. What do you do if you forget your homework?"

He looked confused. "Homework? You mean chores?"

"No, homework. Like, schoolwork that you have to do at home. So the teachers can torture you even when you're not at school."

"Oh. You mean lessons."

"Is that what you call them?"

"Well, if we don't complete our lessons at school, then we have to bring them home."

"Yeah. Homework. It's the pits."

"The pits?"

"The pits, like, you know, a total pain."

"Well, lessons are awfully dull, but they're better than getting a whipping."

"A whipping? Whoa! All we get is demerits. If you get too many you have to stay after school."

I pushed Will toward the door. "Come on. We better get out of here before the doctor comes. Bye. I'll call you tonight," I said to Reuben.

"Thank you," he called out after us.

We passed a nurse in the hall and she stopped us. "You all going to come back again?" she asked.

"Yup," said Will.

"Maybe," I said.

"Well, I sure hope you do. It does him a world of good. Honestly, he was more chipper last night after you left than he has been since he got here. And that's the ticket, you know. You can't get better when you're in the dumps. So you all keep on coming, and he'll soon be out of here."

But where would he go, I wondered. Where would he go?

# 8

WE MADE IT JUST IN TIME for the last school bus. As we climbed on I saw Lori Nelson, a girl in my class, and I sat down beside her. Will sat right behind us. There was no one his age on the bus this late. Most kids had gone home already. There were no sports on Wednesdays, so the only kids who stayed after school were detention kids or kids who stayed for tutoring.

"Why are you guys still here?" Lori asked.

"We had to visit a friend in the hospital, so we just came back to get a ride. How about you?"

"Math tutoring," Lori said, rolling her eyes. "I hate Glick. You're so lucky you don't have her."

"I know. It's bad enough having her for study hall. I couldn't stand having her for math too."

"It's even worse for tutoring. I was the only one there today, and she sat right beside me. The fumes from her perfume almost asphyxiated me."

"Oh, gross. That perfume she wears is so disgusting."

"And the tutoring didn't even help. I still don't get the problems for tonight's homework. How could I concentrate when I could hardly breathe?" Lori opened her backpack and took out her homework. In a minute she was sighing and erasing and saying under her breath, "I hate her, I really hate her."

I took out some work too, but before I could get started I felt a tap on my shoulder.

"What?" I turned back to Will. He nodded toward the other side of the bus. "Look over there," he whispered.

I looked. Gary Richtor sat sprawled across his seat with his dirty boots sticking out into the aisle. "So what? It's just Gary Richtor. He probably had to stay for detention. There's nothing new about that."

"Look what he's got in his hands."

I could see that he was holding something, but I couldn't see what it was. "What is it?" I whispered to Will.

"Shh. You'll see."

As I watched him, he leaned back, resting his head against the window of the bus, and his elbow on the back of the seat, and I could see what he held. It was a pocket watch. A round gold pocket watch. It was exactly the same size as the one Reuben had been holding. Gary held the watch up, turning it around and around in his hands. I tried to see the face of the watch, but I couldn't get a good look at it.

I let a pencil fall from my backpack. It rolled down the aisle toward the back of the bus, and I got up and started after it. Gary was sitting two seats behind us and when I passed his seat I took a good look at the face of the watch.

I understood what Reuben had meant when he said it was a special watch. This sounds crazy, I know, but there was something, well, magical about it. The colors were incredibly bright—vibrant, as our art teacher would say—and there were little paintings of the sun and moon on its face. That was all I had time to see, but it was enough to get the idea. I didn't want Gary to notice that I was looking at it, so I picked up my pencil and started back to my seat. As I passed him, he turned to look at me, and his lips kind of stretched across his face in what I guess was supposed to be a smile.

"How ya doin', babe?" he said, and he slid the watch into the pocket of his tight black pants. I walked on past him, but I knew he was watching me. I could feel his eyes on me. They reminded me of a shark's eyes, black and lifeless.

For the rest of the bus ride I pretended to be reading, but I was thinking. Thinking about that watch. And about everything that Reuben had told us. I still hadn't decided if I believed him or not, but seeing that watch . . . There was something about it. I can't really explain it. All I can tell you is that when I saw it in Gary's heavy, dirty hands I wanted to grab it away from him. There was no doubt in my mind that it was Reuben's, and that Gary had stolen it. But could the watch really do what Reuben said it could?

At the stop before ours Gary came lumbering down the aisle, holding a cigarette. You're not allowed to smoke on the bus, but Gary always lights up just before his stop. He does it to annoy everyone, especially the bus driver. As he passed my seat he flicked my hair with his hand and said, "Later, babe." Then he turned and blew a stream of his disgusting cigarette smoke at me before he swung off the bus.

"Ohh, gross," I screamed, ripping the window open so I wouldn't have to breathe his smoke. "He's so disgusting. And he touched my hair. I'll have to wash it with industrial strength shampoo tonight."

As soon as the bus pulled away from the curb, Will said, "Did you see it? I bet that's Reuben's watch. Where else would he get a watch like that? It has to be the one."

I nodded. "I'm sure it is. I'm going to call Reuben as soon as we get home and get him to describe it, but I'm almost certain that's it. And Gary was on the beach that afternoon. I saw him. When I was waiting for the paramedics, I saw him. When he saw me, he disappeared, as if he had something to hide. I bet he found the watch and took it. Now all we have to do is figure out how we get it back from him."

"I don't like him," Will said with a shiver. "He gives me the creeps."

"I don't like him either, but at least now we know where the watch is. It's better to know. I mean, it could have been at the bottom of the river, and then Reuben would never be able to get home."

Wait a minute, I told myself. I'm talking as though I believe it. As though I really believe that that watch can move people around through time. Oh, great, I thought. I'm getting as crazy as he is.

# 9

IT WAS DUSK when we got off the bus, and the air was cold. As we walked up our drive I could smell chimney smoke, and I knew that Mom had built a fire. A flock of Canada geese passed through the pink glow of the sunset, strung across the sky in gangly, uneven lines, honking and squawking noisily as they flew. It was fall. Summer was gone. Things seemed to be moving fast. So fast I felt kind of dizzy. I stopped to watch the geese, but Will tugged at my sleeve. "Come on, Jess. What are you waiting for?"

Mom was in the kitchen, dressed in jeans and an oversized flannel shirt, flipping through a cookbook. She was wearing a Walkman and singing loudly and totally off key. RESPECT by Aretha Franklin, her favorite. She hadn't noticed that we had come in yet, and I signaled to Will to be quiet. Then I snuck up behind her and lifted the headphones off her head. "Hi, Mom."

Mom spun around. "Oh, lordy, you scared me."

"Sorry, Mom, but you were belting out Aretha, and I knew you couldn't hear us."

Mom took off the headphones and put down the Walkman. She smoothed my hair back, and kissed Will on his forehead. "Well, did you go see our friend? How is he today?"

"He's better," Will told her. "And the nurse said we were the best medicine and asked us to come back as often as we can."

"When will he be getting out of the hospital?"

"They don't know yet," I said. I looked at Will. I wanted to be sure he didn't say too much.

"Still no word from his family?"

I shook my head.

"Poor child. It must be awful for him. Well, I'm glad you two are visiting him. That's something anyway. It's very sweet of you both." Mom went back to the cookbook.

"Something smells good," said Will.

"Lasagna. Eric is coming for dinner, and I want it to be nice. The last few times he's been here we've had Chinese carryout or pizza. I think he thinks we never eat anything that doesn't come in a cardboard box. I'm trying to find the recipe for that Italian salad dressing. I know it was in this cookbook, but I can't remember what they called it. Creamy herb, or herby cream, something like that. Jess, you can wash the lettuce if you want."

I got out the colander and the head of lettuce and began tearing it up. Eric was coming. Of course. That's why Mom was in such a good mood.

"He'll be here in just a few minutes. I'm going to run up and put on a clean shirt. Willy, you could start setting the table for me. Oh, I made an apple pie for dessert too. Look, isn't it beautiful?" Mom took the pie down from the shelf where it was cooling and held it out for us to admire. "Of course, I used a frozen crust, but still it's pretty impressive, don't you think?"

"Yum," said Will.

"Not bad, Mom. It looks almost edible," I said.

She put the pie back on the shelf and hurried out of the kitchen.

"Boy, Mom sure is in a good mood," Will said when she had gone.

"Yeah, I wonder why. Could it possibly have anything to do with the imminent arrival of Eric the Great?"

"I like Eric," said Will.

"He's all right. As long as we don't have to see too much of him," I said.

I finished washing the lettuce and went into the den to call Reuben. I couldn't wait to tell him about the watch. I flopped down on the couch and took out the notebook I had written his number on, and dialed. The phone rang twice and then Reuben answered.

"Jessie?"

"Yeah, it's me. But you're supposed to say 'Hello.' What if it were someone else?"

"I knew no one else would be calling me, so it had to be you. Are you at home? You sound as if you're in the next room."

"That's a telephone. I could be in Japan, and I'd still sound as if I was in the next room."

"It's wonderful," said Reuben. "If I had one of these I'd do nothing but talk all day long."

"You should meet my friend Dana. She does talk all day. Anyway, I've got some news."

"Some news?"

"Yeah. I think we saw your watch."

"You found the watch?" he cried.

"Wait a minute, don't get excited. I said we saw it. At least, I'm almost sure it's yours. But there's a little problem. First of all, tell me what your watch looks like."

He described the colors and the paintings of the sun and moon. "That's it. It has to be it. There can't be more than one watch that looks like that."

"Where is it? Can you bring it to me?"

"Well, that's the problem. See, there's this guy named Gary Richtor who's a real creep. Probably the biggest creep around. He's also our neighbor. And he's got your watch. We saw him on the bus going home, and there he was with this watch. I knew right away when I saw it that it had to be yours. What I think happened is that he found it on the beach the same day we found you. I saw him there, and when he saw me he disappeared. And now he has your watch. So now all we have to do is figure out how to get it back from him."

"Can't we just ask him for it?" asked Reuben.

"Ha. Obviously you've never had the pleasure of meeting Gary. You don't ask Gary for anything. In fact, if he knows we want it, it'll be harder to get it from him. If he finds out how valuable it is, he'll never give it up."

"But it's my watch. He can't just keep it."

"Wanna bet? I told you, the more he thinks we want it, the less likely it is he'll give it up. No, we'll have to think of some other way to get it. Fortunately, Gary's not exactly long on brains, so we should be able to figure out something."

Reuben didn't say anything, so I went on. "Look, at least we know where it is. I mean, it might have been at the bottom of the river for all we knew. We know where it is and we'll get it back. It'll just take some time."

"He's got my watch. He's actually got my watch." I wasn't sure if he was happy to know where it was, or angry that Gary had it. A little of both, I guessed.

"Don't worry, we'll—" I began to reassure him again, but he cut me off.

"Look, I've got to get out of here. I'm going mad in here, and besides, I heard the doctor talking to the nurse a while ago. He said if my memory doesn't come back in a day or two they're going to do a brain scan, whatever that is. Then they talked about calling the juvenile authorities to notify them about my case. Who are the juvenile authorities?"

"I'm not sure, but I have a feeling you don't want to find out. I think they're the guys who figure out what to do with kids no one else knows what to do with."

"That's what I thought. See what I mean? I've got to get out of here."

"Mmm. There's just one problem. Where will you go?"

"Somewhere. Anywhere. I just can't stay here much longer."

Mom called me to tell me dinner was ready. I had heard Eric come in a while ago. "Look, Reuben. Let me think about this. I'll call you tomorrow, okay?"

"All right. Thanks for calling."

I hung up the phone and took a deep breath. The last thing I needed right now was dinner with the lovebirds. If Eric asked me how I felt about something, I'd probably haul off and sock him. I was still trying to make sense of everything Reuben had told me, but it wasn't easy. How can you make sense of something that makes no sense? I dragged myself off the couch. At least we were having lasagna, and I had to admit it smelled great.

When I came into the dining room, they were already sitting down. Mom at one end, Eric on one side of her, and Will on the other. Mom was serving the lasagna, and Eric was helping himself to salad. I went to my own place, and Eric stood up and leaned toward me for a kiss. "Hi, Jess.

You're looking especially pretty this evening. You must have had a good day. Or maybe it's just me. Everything looks good to me today."

Mom passed me a plate of lasagna, and Eric passed the salad.

"Well, did you get that math test back yet?" Eric asked.

"Not yet," I told him.

"Maybe you got an F," Will said.

"I think I did okay," I said.

"Nobody in my class ever gets an *F*," said Will. "Except Christopher Finney. He doesn't really get *F*s, but he has to go out and sit on the bench a lot. Yesterday he threw his grilled cheese sandwich at Marcia Adleson and it got stuck in her hair. She started to cry and Christopher got sent to the bench."

"Hmm. Wild times at Jefferson first grade," I said.

Mom and Eric were both staring at Will while he talked, pretending to be paying attention. But I could tell they were wrapped up in themselves. They looked at each other and smiled this sickening smile.

"That's quite a story, Will. How did you feel about Christopher getting sent to the bench?" asked Eric. There he goes again. He better not ask me how I feel about anything tonight, I thought. I'm not in the mood. I might decide that Christopher Finney had a pretty good idea. I wondered how Eric would look with lasagna stuck in his hair.

"I was glad," said Will. "Marcia is a crybaby some-times, but I wouldn't want a grilled cheese sandwich stuck in my hair."

"No, indeed," said Eric.

"By the way, Will was wondering if you might take him to the game next Saturday," Mom said.

"Next Saturday?" He looked at Mom. "I'm free, aren't I?"

"As far as I know," she said.

"Well, I think that would be great, Willy. I'd love to go with you."

"Okay," Will shouted. And Mom beamed at the two of them.

I guess if I hadn't been so preoccupied by Reuben and the watch, and all, not to mention everything that was going on in school, I would have seen what was coming next, but as it was, it took me completely by surprise. I mean, all the signs were there, and actually, when I think back on it, they had been for a few weeks.

I was caught totally off guard. When Mom took Eric's hand and said, "Kids, there's something we need to talk about," I had no idea what was coming.

I looked at Mom, expecting her to say something about how we've got to remember to hang up the towels in the bathroom, or that we've been tying up the telephone and have to limit our phone calls.

So when she said, "Eric and I have decided to get married," I just stared at her. At first I thought I hadn't heard right, but then I looked at the way Eric held Mom's hand, and the way they looked at each other, and I knew I had heard right. No one said anything. I kept staring at their hands, and for a really weird minute I saw my father's tanned rough hand holding Mom's, instead of Eric's smooth white one. Then I knew that I had to get out of there. I jumped up, shoved back my chair, and ran out of the dining room. I bolted up the stairs to my room, locked the door, and flopped down on the bed; I lay there, feeling the blood pumping through my body, and Mom's words echoing in my head.

# 10

I DON'T KNOW how long I lay there on my bed, staring up at the bottom of my top bunk—the same bunk I've had since I was five years old. As I lay there I started thinking about the day we had bought the bunks. My father had worked all afternoon putting them together, and I had stood behind him handing him the hammer, then the screwdriver, then the wrench, as he asked for them. We had gotten new Mickey Mouse bedspreads for them which I thought were really terrific. When I was eight I told my mother I couldn't stand having Mickey Mouse bedspreads anymore, and we got the ones I still have, which are pink with purple stripes.

But the bottom of the top bunk looked the same way it always had, the same nicks in the wooden slats, the same patterns in the grain of the wood, and the word *why?* that I had written in small black letters a few days after my father was killed. I kept staring at that word *why*. It was what I wanted to ask Mom right then. "Why?" Why was she going to marry Eric? We were just fine, the three of us. Why did we need someone else?

Finally I got up and went over to my desk. I unlocked the bottom drawer, which is the only one that locks. I keep all my valuable things there. That way Will can't get his grubby little paws on them, and Mom can't go snooping through them. I took out a picture of me and my father standing together on the dock. My father was trying to teach me how to catch a crab, and his arms are around me, helping me hold the net. It's funny, I don't really remember that day in particular. It was like so many other days, except that this picture was taken just a couple of weeks before he was killed. I was looking at the picture, trying to remember that day, when there was a knock on the door.

"Who is it?" I said.

"Me," said Will.

I got up, went to the door and unlocked it, and Will opened it. "Can I come in?" he asked.

I shrugged and went back to my desk and sat down again, and Will went over to my bed. He climbed up to the top bunk and sat there, his legs hanging over the side. "Watcha doing?" he asked.

"Nothing much. Just looking through some old stuff."

"How come you ran away from the table like that? Mom was pretty upset. After you left she got up and went out to the kitchen. When she came back her face was all red. I think she might have been crying," he said.

Brilliant deduction, Sherlock, I thought, but I didn't say anything. I knew I couldn't explain it to Will. It wasn't that I wanted to hurt Mom, or even Eric . . . it was just . . . "I don't know, Willy. I just don't want everything to change. I mean, we're okay as it is. Why does she have to go and upset everything?"

I was holding the picture of me and Dad, and Will looked at it.

"That's Dad and you, isn't it," he asked, leaning down from the bed to get a better look. I nodded.

"Are there any of me and him?"

"I don't know. Maybe Mom has one. You could ask her."

"Do you think Dad would mind? Is that why you don't want Mom and Eric to get married?"

"Dad's dead, Will. And anyway, he would want Mom to be happy." As I said it, I knew it was true. Dad would have wanted Mom to be happy. No, it wasn't that. That wasn't the reason I didn't want them to get married.

"Are you going to come back down and eat dinner? There's pie for dessert, remember."

I shook my head. "I'm not that hungry. You can go down, though."

"I already finished. The pie was really good. You should try it."

"I'll be down in a little while, Willy. You go on."

Will jumped down from the top bed, landing on his hands and knees on my rug. He turned a somersault in the direction of the door. "Open the door," he said. "I'm going to somersault all the way back to my room."

I opened the door for him and he rolled out into the hall.

I was still sitting at my desk when there was another knock.

"It's me, honey. Can we talk?" Mom. I shoved the picture back in my drawer and slammed it shut.

"It's not locked," I said.

She came in and sat on the end of the bed. She noticed my backpack and said, "Do you have a lot of homework tonight?"

I shrugged.

Mom looked down at her hands. She began twisting her rings, the rings that Dad had given her. She always does that when she's nervous.

"Jess, I . . . I'm sorry. I guess I should have talked to you privately. I didn't mean to spring it on you like that. It's just that Eric and I are both so happy, and so excited, and it never occurred to me that you and Will wouldn't feel the same way I do. I guess that was pretty foolish of me, and I . . . I'm sorry."

"But you're still getting married?" I asked.

"Yes. Yes. We're still going to get married. And I know, I understand now, that this may be difficult for you, but . . . I love Eric, Jess, and he loves me. And he loves you too. I really thought you liked him. He's certainly tried hard with both of you."

"It's not that I don't like him, Mom."

"Then what? What is it? Can you tell me?"

I shrugged. I started picking at the bedspread, pulling at a string from it. What could I tell her? That I didn't like the way he always asked me how I felt about things? That I didn't like the idea that someone who was practically a stranger was going to move right into our house, into our family? That the only person I wanted acting like my father was my father, and that he was dead? I couldn't tell her all that, so I just kept on picking at the bedspread until Mom put her hand over mine and said, "Don't, honey. You'll pull the whole thing apart."

Then the phone rang. Will raced to get it and in a minute he was shouting for Mom.

She stood up. "I'll be right there," she called. She smoothed my hair back from my forehead. "Sweetie, I know this is a big change, and I really am sorry I didn't talk with you first. But please, do try. Give Eric a chance. For me, for all of us. He deserves a chance, don't you think?"

I nodded because there was nothing else to do. It was obvious Mom wasn't going to change her mind. When she left I went back over to my desk and took out the picture of me and Dad.

# 11

THE NEXT MORNING when I first woke up I thought for a minute that maybe I had dreamed everything that had happened the day before. The whole thing about Reuben and about Mom and Eric. I mean, you have to admit, it's a lot for one day, to find out that a kid you know has been zipping through time with a magic watch, and that your mother is getting remarried. It's no wonder I felt a little weird. But after I lay in bed for a while I knew that none of it had been a dream. I sat up and stretched and looked out the window. It was a beautiful fall morning, the sun dancing on the water and the geese squawking. I sat there for a long time, looking out the window and thinking about everything that had been happening lately.

I remembered that I had a soccer game after school that day, which was good because it gave me the perfect excuse not to go see Reuben. After what he had told us I kind of needed a break. I wanted to see him, but, I don't know, the whole thing was just so weird. I still needed some time to think about it.

So anyway, this game was one of the most important of the season. If we won it would mean we made the play-offs, so naturally, everyone was pretty psyched up and intense. All day in school it was all anyone could talk about, which was also good, because it kept my mind off everything else.

I play second-string center halfback, and most of the time I don't see too much action because Sally Wells, the first-string center half is one of the fastest players on the team. When they take her out and put me in, everyone groans—I'm not kidding. Since this game was so impor-tant, I was pretty sure I wouldn't be playing much at all, and I wouldn't have, except that in the first five minutes of the game Sally fell and sprained her ankle. Out she comes and in I go, and everyone's practically in tears thinking, oh no, with Sally out and Jessie in, there's no hope for winning. I have to admit I agreed with them, especially that day, since I had a few other things on my mind besides the game. Mom usually tries to get to my games, especially if they're important like this one, but she had told me that she had a faculty meeting that afternoon, and that she would have to miss the game. So, when I looked over at the sidelines a couple minutes after I'd been put in, and saw Will waving to me, I was surprised. How had he gotten there? Maybe Mom's meet-ing had been canceled, I thought.

Then I saw Eric standing on one side of the bleachers talking to one of the other fathers. Eric must have brought Will. Had he come just to see me play? I wondered. I thought of the times I had envied the other girls whose fathers came and cheered for them from the sidelines. The fathers were always louder and more excited in the stands than the mothers. The mothers mostly just talked among themselves and didn't really pay much attention to the game, but the fathers yelled and cheered, and took it all very seriously. Did Eric really care about my game, or was he just trying to get me to like him so he could marry Mom without a fuss?

Well, either way, I decided, I wasn't going to let him see me mess up. We were down by one goal when the center from the other team broke down the field with the ball. I went after her and stopped her just in time. I stole the ball and passed it to the left wing, Shelby Bloom, who took it down the field and scored. Now the game was tied and the crowd in the bleachers went crazy. I could see Eric yelling and clapping. I wondered if he'd seen my play.

The score stayed tied until the last two minutes of the game, when we scored. When the game ended, we had won. We were going to the play-offs. Naturally everyone on the team and in the stands went wild, hugging and cheering and slapping each other.

Finally we all calmed down, and I was walking off the field with Dana and Cynthia. "Isn't that Eric?" Dana asked. "Did he come to watch?"

I nodded. "He brought Will. Mom couldn't come because she had a faculty meeting." Eric was heading toward us, and I whispered to Dana, "I've got something to tell you."

Then Eric was there. He put his arm around my shoulders and said, "Great game, girls. You guys really played your hearts out."

Will ran up and grabbed me. "You were good," he said. "You didn't score any goals, but you still played good. Better than usual."

"Thanks, Willy."

"Listen," Eric said, "I'm going to drive Will home. Do you want us to wait for you?" Eric asked.

"That's okay. I'll get a ride home with Dana." I looked at Dana, who nodded. "But thanks. And . . . thanks for coming."

"Hey, I wouldn't have missed it," he said, and he stood there like he wanted to say something else, but Dana and Cynthia were waiting for me. "Well, I gotta go change. See you later." Eric nodded, and he and Will walked off toward the parking lot.

"What did you want to tell me?" Dana asked.

"They're getting married. Mom and Eric. They told us last night at dinner."

"You're kidding! Your mother and Eric? Wow! When?"

I shrugged. "I don't think they've chosen a date yet, but it's definite."

"You don't seem too happy. Don't you like him? He seems okay to me."

How could I explain it? Even Dana, my best friend, who understands everything about me, wouldn't understand.

"Yeah. He's okay. It's just, oh, I don't know."

"Well, at least he's not Mr. Fit. Or the plumber. I mean, let's face it. It could be worse."

"Yeah. It could be worse. Eric's not a bad guy. It's just that . . . " Then the door of the locker room flew open and everyone was grabbing us and pulling us into the party that was going on.

When everyone got tired of celebrating, we changed out of our uniforms and went out to the parking lot to meet Dana's mother.

Mrs. Andrews is this tiny dark-haired woman, full of energy and really talkative. She's some kind of scientist and works for an environmental organization. I'm not sure exactly what she does, but she's really committed to her work. I like her a lot, even though Dana and I sometimes laugh at her, especially when she gets going on one of her scientific lectures.

"You girls were marvelous," Mrs. Andrews said as we drove to my house. "I just love to watch those games. It's wonderful, the way you can make that ball go where you want it to."

Dana looked at me and rolled her eyes. "It's really not that hard, Mom."

"Well, it looks hard to me. I never played sports much when I was young, but when I watch you girls out there it looks like such fun, and I think maybe I missed something. I guess I was always too busy studying." She paused, and then added, "I did belong to the science club though."

"The science club. Gee, that sounds pretty exciting, Mom," Dana said, giving me another look.

"Oh, we did have an awful lot of fun," said her mother.

"What did you do, like, have frog-dissecting parties? Bring your own petri dish?"

"Oh, stop making fun of me. We did all kinds of things."

"I think I'll stick to the soccer team, if it's okay with you, Mom."

"Well, judging by your last science grade, I think that's probably for the best," said her mother.

Before Dana could come up with an answer, her mother pulled up in front of my house, and I climbed out. "Thanks, Mrs. Andrews."

"I'll call you later," said Dana.

I slammed the car door and went up the walk to the house. Inside, Mom was at her desk grading papers.

"Hi, sweetie. I just got home a few minutes ago, and I have mounds of work tonight. Tell me about the game?"

"We won, five-four. We made the play-offs."

"I know. Will told me. I'm thrilled. And it sounds like it was an exciting game. I'm sorry I had to miss it. And the faculty meeting was nothing but a waste of time. Everyone whining and complaining about curriculum changes and scheduling problems."

"Well, you can come to the play-offs," I told her.

"I wouldn't miss them," Mom said. "Listen, honey. There's some chicken in the oven for dinner. Would you be a love and make a salad? It's just us three tonight."

"Eric's not here?" I asked. I knew I would have to talk to him sooner or later, but I didn't want it to be tonight.

"No. He had to go back to work. Oh, and listen, honey. Eric has to go back up to Boston on business next week, and he's asked me to come with him to meet his sister. She lives just outside Boston. It's midterm break at the college, so it works out beautifully. We're leaving Saturday and we'll be back by the middle of the week."

"Saturday? That's the day after tomorrow."

"I know. I know it's short notice, but it all came together so nicely, and I do want to meet his sister. She sounds terrific, and Eric's very close to her. I checked with Daphne and she said she'd be glad to stay. She'll have a lot of studying, of course, but she'll be able to get you wherever you need to go, and look after everything."

"Oh. Well, okay." Daphne's one of Mom's students. She had begun babysitting for us three years ago when she was a freshman, and now she's a senior. She stays with us whenever Mom has to go away. She's kind of flaky, but we like her.

"I won't miss your play-offs, will I?"

"No. They don't start for another two weeks." Mom went back to her papers, and I said, "I guess I'll go make the salad."

"Thanks, hon. The chicken should be about done, so we can eat as soon as you're finished."

The phone rang in the middle of dinner and I answered it.

"Jessie? It's Reuben. Can you hear me?"

"Of course I can hear you. Sorry we couldn't come today, but I had a soccer game."

"Oh. I thought maybe you weren't going to come anymore. Listen. There's something I have to talk to you about."

"We're in the middle of dinner. Can I call you in about ten minutes?"

"Oh. All right. Sorry to interrupt."

"That's okay. At least you're not selling something."

"What?"

"Never mind. Look, I'll call you in a few minutes."

I hung up and went back to the table. I finished up quickly, took my plate out to the kitchen and washed it, and then went upstairs to call Reuben back. I was curious. What did he have to talk to me about?

When he heard my voice he said, "Oh, Jessie. Thank you for calling me back. As I said, I've got to talk to you. I . . . I've got to get out of here. There's not much time left. I overheard the nurse talking to the social worker today. They're going to move me to a juvenile center soon. They're talking about a foster home or something. Jessie, you've got to help me get out of here. I can't stay here. I've got to get my watch back and get home."

His voice sounded kind of funny, like he was just about to panic, but was trying really hard not to.

"Listen, calm down. I'll help you," I said to reassure him. "We'll get you out. But you can't just walk out, can you? Wouldn't someone stop you?"

"I think if I do it around lunchtime, when all the nurses are very busy, I can make it. And I'll go out the back door. There's a garden back there that the patients are allowed to sit in. If I can get out there, I can just wait for the right moment and climb over the fence."

"And then what?" I asked him.

"I don't know. All I know is I have to find this boy who has my watch and get it back."

"Finding him won't be a problem. But getting the watch from him will be. I'm telling you, the guy is a creep. It's going to take some time. And some planning."

"Well, all I know is I have to get out of here. Once I'm out, I can plan what to do next."

"But where will you go? And what if they look for you? Maybe the hospital will notify the police that you're missing."

Reuben didn't say anything for a minute. "Do you think they will?"

"Probably. They must have to do something. And anyway, where will you stay? You could stay here, but then we'd have to tell Mom all about it . . . "

"We can't do that. You know we can't."

He was right. Mom would never believe it. She'd have us committed if we tried to tell her that Reuben was from another century. I picked up a pen that was lying near the phone and began doodling, drawing a watch like Reuben's.

And then I remembered what Mom had told me. About her trip with Eric. "Wait a minute," I said. "I'm getting an idea. Look, my Mom is going away the day after tomorrow. She'll be gone about five days. That should give us time . . . "

"You mean I could stay at your house?"

"Why not? We'll tell Daphne you're a cousin, or, or a friend of Dana's. I'll think of something. Daphne believes anything. Last time Mom went away we told her that Dana had to stay with us because her mother was conducting a science experiment, and if it didn't work it would blow her house up. And she believed it. Dana got to stay over for the whole three days. So she'll believe this one, I'm sure.

"Wait," said Reuben. "I'm confused. Dana's your friend, right? But who's Daphne?"

I explained about Daphne. "So. It'll work just fine. Trust me. Now, I'll come in tomorrow and bring anything you need. What about clothes? Can you get your clothes?"

"I think they hung them in the closet here. Wait, I'll check." He put the phone down. While he was gone I thought about what I was doing. Was I nuts? Why was I doing this? The guy might be a lunatic for all I knew. And here I was, letting him stay in our house. Part of me knew it was crazy, but the other part of me trusted him. I wanted to help. There was nothing else I could do.

In a minute he was back on the line. "Yes. Everything's here, my knickers, and the oilskins."

"Knickers and oilskins? Wait a minute. You can't wear that. You won't even make it out of the hospital in those clothes. I'll have to get you some jeans. Let me see, mine would be too small . . . maybe I could buy some, or—I know —Dana's brother Brendan is about your size. Maybe we can borrow some from him. Hold on a minute, Mom's calling me."

"What, Mom?" I shouted.

"I need to use the phone. Can you wrap it up?"

"Listen, I've got to go. But I'll come in tomorrow and bring the clothes. The next day is Saturday, and Mom will be gone, so you can come here, and then we'll figure out how we're going to get your watch back."

"All right. I'll see you tomorrow, then."

"Right."

I hung up quickly and called down to tell Mom that the line was free. Back in my own room I sat on my bed and thought about what I should tell Dana. I needed her help to get the jeans, but I couldn't tell her the truth. Dana had a big mouth sometimes. She'd never be able to keep it a secret.

While I thought about it I looked out the window, and I saw Gary down on the beach. He had his dog, a pit bull terrier, with him on a tight leash, the kind of leash attached to a collar with spikes on it. When he jerked the leash, the collar dug into the dog's neck. Gary commanded the dog to sit, and took something out of his jacket. At first I couldn't see what it was, then I saw that it was a BB gun. While I watched he took aim at a sea gull and shot it. The sea gull's wing was injured and it dropped to the ground, hopping about, trying to fly. Then Gary released his dog, who caught the bird and shook it until it hung limp and dead. Oh, what a sicko, I thought. He gets his kicks watching sea gulls die.

What happened next was even creepier. This sounds really strange, but I swear it happened. Gary reached into his pocket again, and this time he pulled out the watch —Reuben's watch. Then he turned and looked right at me, even though I knew he couldn't see me, and couldn't know that I was watching him. But he looked right at my window, and I'll never forget the expression on his face. It still gives me the shivers to think about it, even now. Before I knew what I was doing I reached over and pulled down the shade on my window, trying to shut out that horrible face.

# 12

I KNEW I WASN'T GOING to get any homework done that night. There was too much else to think about. I opened my backpack and pulled out my books, but that was as far as I got. The first thing I had to do was call Dana. I had to get Reuben some clothes to wear besides his own stuff. I could just see him walking around town in knickers and oilskins.

When Dana answered, I said, "Listen, I need to borrow a pair of Brendan's jeans. Can you get some for me? I need them tomorrow."

"Huh? Why do you need a pair of Brendan's jeans?"

"It's kind of complicated."

"If you want the jeans, you better tell me why."

I had known Dana would want to know what was going on, and I had decided to tell her about Reuben wanting to get out of the hospital, but nothing about the watch, or the time traveling.

"Well, you know the boy we found on the beach? Reuben Miller?"

"The one you've been going to see in the hospital?"

"Yeah."

"Yeah, what about him?"

"Well, the jeans are for him. He's sneaking out of the hospital. He can't stay in there any longer."

"But I thought he had amnesia."

"He does, but they're going to move him to some kind of juvenile center, and he wants to get out before they do."

"But where's he going to go?"

"He's coming here. Mom and Eric are going away, up to Boston to see Eric's sister, and Daphne's staying with us. We'll just tell her he's a friend who's visiting. I'll think of something. You know Daphne. She'll believe anything."

"Yeah, but what about when your Mom comes back?"

"Oh, he'll be gone by then. He's just staying a few days, until he can figure some things out."

"Is he cute? When do I get to meet him?"

"You can meet him after he gets to our house. And yeah, he is kind of cute."

"I knew it. I knew you had a crush on him. Why else would you spend practically every afternoon visiting him?"

"Dana. I don't have a crush on him. It's just that . . . I just want to help him, that's all."

"Yeah, sure. Well, I'll get you the jeans, but you owe me."

"Great. Bring them to school tomorrow. I'll take them to him tomorrow afternoon."

"Okay. What about shoes. Doesn't he need shoes?"

"Hmm. I forgot about shoes. Does Brendan have an extra pair of sneakers you could get?"

"Yeah. There must be an old pair lying around somewhere. I'll bring them too."

"Okay. Thanks, Dana. See you tomorrow."

I wanted to get her off the phone before she asked any more questions. I hung up, thinking that that was one problem taken care of. Now all I had to do was come up with a logical story to tell Daphne about who Reuben was once he got here. Then we could work on the big problem—how to get the watch away from Gary.

The next day, as soon as school was out, I walked back to the hospital, carrying the paper bag with jeans and sneakers that Dana had given me that morning, and a big sweatshirt that I had in my closet. I was kind of nervous as I walked past the nurses' station. I thought I saw them looking curiously at the bag, but maybe I was just imagining it. I mean, there's no law against carrying a bag in a hospital. I hurried past the desk and went down the hall and knocked on Reuben's door.

"Come in," he called.

I went in, closing the door behind me. "I've got everything. I just hope they fit," I told him, handing him the bag.

He looked in the bag. "Good. I'll go try them on." He went into the bathroom and in a few minutes he came out wearing the clothes I had brought him. He looked at me with an embarrassed expression. "How do I look?" he asked.

I stared when I saw him, he looked so . . . different. "You . . . you look just like a regular kid," I said. "I mean . . ."

Reuben laughed, "You mean not like some fossil from the last century?"

I had to admit, he looked good. He really was cute, not Roger Simms type of cute, but cute all the same.

"Well, that hospital gown didn't do much for you," I told him.

"So this is what boys wear now?" he asked.

I nodded. "Except when they get dressed up. Then they wear a jacket and tie. Does everything fit okay?"

"I think so. I just have to get used to them."

"Well, tomorrow's the big day, right? What time should I meet you?" I asked him.

I think I can sneak out of here about 12:15, when the nurse is busy getting lunch served. I'll go down to the garden, and then, when the coast is clear, I'll just climb the fence."

"Okay, I'll meet you at 12:30 on the corner across the street from the hospital. I think Dana's sister can give us a ride, and, if not, we can take the bus."

"The bus. You keep talking about the bus. What is a bus?"

"Jeez. You've got a lot to learn. A bus is . . . like a big car that carries a lot of people. If Dana's sister can't get the car, we'll take a bus."

"And a car is an automobile, right?"

I just stared at him. I didn't know if this was going to work. Even Daphne was going to be suspicious of someone who doesn't know what a car is.

"Yes. Have you ever ridden in one?"

He shook his head. "I've heard about them. Will I get to ride in one tomorrow?"

"Probably. If Dana's sister can get the car," I said again. I was getting tired of telling him that. "Everyone has cars now. Some families have two or three."

"Is it fun? To ride in a car?"

"Fun? Well, I don't know. It's just a way of getting somewhere. I mean, I think it would be a lot more fun to ride in a horse-drawn carriage, but that's because I never get to do it."

"Yes, but an automobile. How fast does it go?"

He was really getting excited about this car ride, and I was getting more and more worried. I was beginning to see that this might be more complicated than I had thought.

"Look, Reuben, don't worry about the car, okay? We've got a lot to think about. There's going to be a lot of new stuff out there that you've never seen, and you've got to convince everyone you're just a normal kid. It might not be easy."

He sat on the bed and looked down at the floor. "I know. I . . . Jessie, I haven't even thanked you, for these, and for everything. I don't know what I would do if it weren't for you . . . I don't want to be any trouble. If you don't want me to stay with you I'll just sleep outside. If you can just show me where to find the boy who has my watch."

"Wait a minute. I never said I didn't want you to stay with us. I just said don't go getting all excited about a ride in a car when there's a lot of other things to think about. I want you to stay with us, okay?"

There was a knock on the door, and he jumped up. "I've got to get out of these clothes," he whispered. "You can let them in while I change." He bolted for the bathroom and shut the door tightly behind him.

I opened the door and the nurse came in with his dinner tray. "Dinnertime already?" I said.

"Quarter to five. We like to get 'em fed early. That's always the way in hospitals. Where's our friend?" she asked.

Reuben came out of the bathroom dressed in his hospital gown and bathrobe. "I'm hungry. Anything good tonight?" he asked her.

"Now that's a good sign. You eat it all up, and they'll soon let you out of here."

She left the tray on the stand by his bed and went out of the room.

"Look, I've got to go or I'll miss my bus. I'll meet you on the corner across the street from the hospital at 12:30 tomorrow. If anything comes up, call me. Otherwise, I'll be there, okay?"

"All right." He looked at his tray of food and made a face. "It'll be nice to be out of here."

# 13

THE NEXT DAY at 12:25 I stood on the corner near the hospital and waited. I had made sure to get there early because I wanted to be there before Reuben. I had a feeling he would be pretty overwhelmed when he stepped out of the hospital into the twentieth century. I didn't want him wandering around by himself.

I had fixed it with Dana that she and her sister Eve would drop me on the corner. Dana and Eve were going to go on to the mall, and Reuben and I would walk down there to meet them.

I stood on the corner watching people coming and going in and out of the hospital. I felt kind of dumb just standing there, and I kept imagining that everyone was looking at me and wondering what I was waiting for. I knew I was just being paranoid, but I couldn't help it. Finally I began walking up and down the sidewalk, just for something to do. At 12:35 I began to get worried.

Where was he? Had something happened? Had the nurses caught him wearing his clothes under his bathrobe? Had someone seen him climbing the fence? By 12:40 I was a mess. What a stupid plan. How could we ever have thought it would work? I was imagining all the things that could have gone wrong when I saw him running toward me.

I waved and waited until he was standing beside me puffing from his run. "You're late. Where've you been?"

"Sorry, but the nurse who comes in to take my blood pressure and temperature was late, so I couldn't change. Usually she comes around 11:30, but today it was almost 12:30. I was going mad. I was just about to change anyway, and then she came. So then I had to get changed, get down to the garden, and then wait until it was all clear. But anyway, here I am."

He stopped and looked around, as if noticing his surroundings for the first time.

"Wow! This is . . . . I've been watching this road from my window, imagining what it's like out here, and now that I'm here . . . . " He shook his head. "It's very different from my world. The cars . . . and . . . . "

He looked around, and his expression reminded me of the way Will looked the first time we took him to Wonderworld Amusement Park. "I guess things have changed a lot in a hundred years."

"I'll say." He jumped back as a car whizzed by. "How fast did you say they go?" he asked.

"Cars can go up to 80 or 90 miles an hour. But the speed limit is 55. Around here it's about 40. Look, we better get going. We have to go meet Dana and Eve, that's her sister, at Record Town in five minutes.

"Record Town? Where is that? Is it far? How can we get to another town in five minutes?"

I laughed. "It's not a town, it's a store that sells tapes and CDs. It's in the mall, just down the road. Come on."

"What are tapes and CDs? And what's a mall?"

I groaned. "You need a crash course in the 1990s. Just remember to watch what you say around other people, or they're really going to wonder about you. Tapes and CDs are like records." He still looked blank. "You know, music that's recorded? You must have records."

"You mean for the phonograph?"

"Yeah, that's right. Only today we have tape players and CD players. Same idea, though."

"And where is this store?"

"In the mall, a few blocks down. A mall is like a big building with lots of stores inside. You'll see."

As we walked I said, "Now look. Dana knows about how we found you and how you were in the hospital and all. I had to tell her I was helping you get out, and she thinks you still have amnesia, so if you mess up we can just blame it on that."

He nodded, but he was still looking around with a slightly dazed air. I didn't know how much he was taking in. As soon as we got inside the mall he stopped and stared.

It's a new mall, and it's pretty extravagant. Lots of plants and white marbly walls and a big fountain in the middle. "What is this place?" he asked.

"I told you, it's a shopping mall. Lots of stores and places to eat."

"But it's so . . . fancy. I've never seen a place like it."

I took the sleeve of his sweatshirt and hauled him along. "We're late. They're going to leave without us if we don't hurry. Come on. Record Town is up this way."

He wanted to stop and look in every store we passed, but I kept us moving. When we came to Record Town I saw Dana and Eve at the cash register.

"There you are," Dana said when she saw me. "We were just wondering where you were."

"Dana, Eve, this is Reuben. Reuben, this is Dana and Eve."

"Hi, Reuben. Jessie's told me all about you," said Dana. She looked at the bandage on his forehead and gasped, "Gosh, look at that. No wonder you have amnesia . . . . " She clapped her hand over her mouth. "Oh, umm, I mean . . . . Oh, I'm sorry."

"That's all right. My memory is beginning to come back. I just need a few more days . . . . But I couldn't stand the hospital anymore. I had to get out of there."

"I don't blame you. Eve was in the hospital once, weren't you, Eve. She had to have her tonsils out. She hated it. She threw a bowl of ice cream at one of the nurses. At least that's what Mom said. I wasn't born, and Eve was only three. She hardly remembers it."

I could tell that Dana was nervous. She always talks a lot when she's nervous. "Did you buy anything?" I asked her.

"I don't have any money. But Eve bought the new Whitney Houston. It's great. And she's going to let me borrow it whenever I want because she's such a nice sister, right, Eveie?"

"Dream on, twerp. Come on, let's get a hamburger at McDonald's. I'm starved."

Reuben was staring at the posters on the walls. He seemed particularly interested in the Rolling Stones and Hammer.

"Do you like the Rolling Stones?" Eve asked, seeing him looking at the posters.

"Uh, oh yes. Yes. They're . . . great."

"Which album do you like best?"

He looked at me and then said quickly. "Umm, I like them all."

"Yeah, me too."

We left Record Town and Eve said, "There's McDonald's. Come on." She went up to the counter and ordered a Big Mac, fries, and a Coke. Then she looked at Reuben. "Know what you want?"

"Umm, I'm not hungry. I already had lunch."

"I'll just have fries and a Coke," I said.

Dana ordered the same. We got our stuff and went to sit down. Reuben was looking around as if he'd never seen a McDonald's before, which of course he hadn't, but Dana and Eve didn't know that. I offered him some fries. He ate one and said, "Those are good."

"Don't they have McDonald's in . . . where are you from anyway?"

"Virginia," I said, at exactly the same time Reuben said, "Massachusetts."

"Well, he used to be from Virginia but he just moved to Massachusetts.

"So, will you be staying long?" Eve asked.

"I don't think so. Just a few days."

When Eve finished her food she said, "Well, gang, we better get going because Mom wants the car back by 2:00. Everyone ready?"

"Be prepared to take your life in your hands," Dana said.

"Eve just got her license a few days ago," I explained to Reuben.

"Hey, any more cracks like that and you can walk home."

"Just kidding," said Dana.

When we got to the car Eve unlocked it and I opened the back door and motioned for Reuben to climb in. He looked excited and a little scared. I just hoped he would keep his mouth shut and not say anything suspicious.

As soon as we got in the car Dana turned around in her seat to look at me. "Have you done the French homework yet?" she asked. "I can't stand Mademoiselle Chenille. Do you know what she did yesterday? You won't believe this. I go up to her after class to tell her I don't understand, and she says, 'Come to tutoring, eef you dun't unnerstan, you come to tutoring.' So after lunch I go to tutoring and she says, 'Why are you here? You are always here. You come too much to tutoring.' The woman is crazy. She tells me to go to tutoring, I go to tutoring and she asks me what I'm doing there. Can you believe that?" Dana demanded, looking at Reuben. He shook his head, which was all the response Dana needed to start her off on another tirade.

"And she always gives me the same grade—72, always 72, no matter how many I miss. I think she'd give me a 72 even if I got them all right. I tell you, the woman is crazy."

Reuben was smiling and nodding as Dana continued to rant about Mademoiselle Chenille. Good, I thought. If Dana does all the talking, Reuben won't have a chance to say anything weird.

In a few minutes we had turned up Cedar Road. "You want me to drop you at your house?" Eve asked.

"Yes, please."

Reuben was sitting up looking at the steering wheel and the dash, trying to see what Eve was doing. I could tell he was fascinated by the car. I guess I would be too if it was my first car ride. In a minute Eve pulled up in front of my house. "I'll call you later," I said to Dana as we slid out of the back seat. "Thanks for the ride, Eve."

"No problem," she called and they drove off.

Reuben looked up at the house. "So this is where you live? I've tried to imagine it as I lay in that bed in the hospital."

"Is this how you pictured it?" I asked.

Reuben tilted his head to one side, looking up at our grey shingled house, and behind it to the river, which was shining in the bright October sun. "Of course, I didn't picture it looking exactly like this, but—I knew it would be nice." I was about to take him inside when we heard an airplane in the distance. Reuben looked around. "What's that?" he asked.

"It's just a plane," I told him. "There it is." I pointed to it as it flew over.

Reuben looked up and at first he flinched and put his hands up over his head, as if to shield himself. Then he just stared as the plane disappeared.

"So it really happened. There really are aeroplanes, just as my grandfather wrote." He shook his head in amazement. "Have you—have you ridden in one?"

"Sure. Lots of times. My grandparents live in Cleveland, so sometimes we fly there to visit them. And two years ago we flew to Florida. That was the best because we were on a plane that had a movie. The food is really gross, though, most of the time."

"Wasn't it frightening? Being up so high with nothing to . . . ."

"Nah. You don't even think about it once you're up there. It's just like a train, really, only it's up in the air.

Come on. Let's go in. I'll introduce you to Daphne. Remember, she thinks you're Dana's cousin, so don't blow it. There's no room in her house, so you have to stay here. Got it?"

I took him around to the back door and into the kitchen. Daphne was there, sitting at the kitchen counter reading one of Will's Spiderman comic books. "Hi, guys," she said. "You must be Reuben, Dana's cousin, right?"

"Yes. That's right," said Reuben, putting out his hand. "Reuben Miller."

"Well, hi, Reuben. I'm Daphne, the babysitter, but I guess Jessie told you that, right?"

"Yes. She told me," he said.

"Well, I'm glad you're here, the more the merrier, as my grandmother always says." She looked puzzled for a minute and then said, "Didn't Dana have a cousin staying with her last time I was here?"

"Uh, yes, but that was another one. From her father's side. Dana has a very big family."

"Oh, I see."

"And a very small house," I added.

"Well, there's plenty of room here," said Daphne. "And besides, the more opinions I get on dinner tonight, the better."

"I thought you'd given up macrobiotics," I said. Daphne was always making these experimental foods for us to try.

"Oh, I did. But now I'm studying ecology, and we're learning how to cook to conserve. We're having seaweed au gratin tonight. You'll love it."

I looked at Reuben. "Don't worry. We'll order a pizza. Come on. You're going to sleep in Will's room. I'll show you where to put your stuff and then we'll go down to the beach."

# 14

"YOU WERE RIGHT HERE. This is the exact spot," I told Reuben.

"I found you," Will said. "I saw your foot first. Your boot was sticking out here, and I almost tripped over it. Then I looked up in the reeds, and saw the rest of you." He shivered, remembering. "I was scared. I thought maybe you were . . . dead or something. I ran down the beach to Jessie, really fast. Didn't I, Jessie?"

I nodded. Reuben stared at the spot, shaking his head. "I don't remember anything. Nothing. I was on the *Lady,* that's my uncle's oyster boat, the *Lady Sarah,* and then I was in the hospital. Nothing in between." He sat down on the sand and stared out at the river. A gull flew by, swooping out over the water and then returning to land on top of a piling of the dock nearby. "It's funny. From here the view is exactly the same. This is what I was looking at from the boat the afternoon before the storm. It looks so familiar. Just the way it looked a hundred years ago, as long as you're looking out at the river."

I sat down on the sand near him, and Will wandered up into the reeds, looking for shells and beach glass. A motorboat came into view, heading down the river toward the Bay. "Of course, we don't have any boats like that." He smiled, watching it. "I'd love a ride in one of those," he said.

"We used to have one, when my dad was alive," I told him, "but he was killed in a motorboat accident. Now all we have is a sailboat."

"How old were you when he died?" he asked.

"It was four years ago. I was nine. Will was only two. He doesn't remember him at all."

Reuben was tracing shapes in the sand with his finger. "I can't imagine having either of my parents die. It must have been awful."

I shrugged. "I guess it was pretty awful. And now my mom is getting remarried."

"Are you glad?" he asked.

I picked up a handful of sand and let it sift through my fingers. "I don't know," I said. "At first I was angry. But now, I don't know. Eric is . . . okay. I mean, he's really pretty nice. And he tries hard. But . . . he's not my dad."

Reuben nodded, and for a minute we were both quiet, lost in our own thoughts. Then I saw a movement up the beach, and I grabbed the sleeve of Reuben's sweatshirt. "There he is. That's Gary. He's got that pit bull with him."

Reuben sat up and put his hand up to his forehead to shade his eyes.

"Why does he keep yanking on that poor dog like that?" Reuben asked.

"He's training him to kill sea gulls."

Reuben looked at me. "Why would he do that?"

"I told you. He's sick. There's no point in asking why he does any of the things he does."

Gary disappeared back into the reeds again, and Reuben said, "How do we get my watch back?"

I shrugged. "It's not going to be easy."

"Can't we just ask him for it? Maybe he doesn't know who it belongs to. If we explain that it's my watch, he might give it back," said Reuben.

I shook my head. It was obvious he didn't understand what kind of person we were dealing with. "I already told you. The more he thinks we want it, the less chance there is we'll get it. If he finds out how valuable it is . . . well, he'll never give it up."

Reuben frowned and shook his head slowly. "I can't stand knowing he has it . . . knowing it's that close. I'm going to ask him for it."

I looked at him. I could see that nothing I said would change his mind. He had to find out for himself what kind of person Gary was. "You can try," I said, but I knew it was hopeless.

He stood up. "It can't hurt to ask. You wait here. I'm going to talk to him."

Reuben walked off up the beach toward the spot where we had seen Gary. I watched until he disappeared into the reeds, and then I waited. In a few minutes he was back, and I knew as he walked toward me that he had not been successful. There was a look on his face I hadn't seen before, a dark, hard look of anger, disappointment, and determination.

It didn't seem like the time to say "I told you so," so I said nothing, and he flopped down in the sand beside me. "I see what you mean."

I nodded. "He's such a creep."

"He . . . he's . . . despicable."

"So what'd he say?"

"Well, I introduced myself as your cousin, and I told him I'd lost my watch. I asked if he might have seen it. And he said, 'What makes you think I've seen it?' So I said, 'Well, actually, my cousin thinks she saw it in your possession.' Then he gave me a very odd look, and he said, 'The only watch she's seen me with is my watch. Got that?' Then he pulled on his dog and the dog started growling at me. I guess that's another little trick he's taught the poor animal. You were right. We're not going to get anywhere with him."

I nodded.

"What about his parents?" Reuben asked. "Do you think we could ask them if they've seen the watch? Maybe they'll make him give it back."

"I guess we could ask his mother, although she doesn't seem like the type who would make Gary do anything. And there's no point in asking his father. He's never home anyway."

"Well, it can't hurt to ask her. If she's seen the watch she must wonder where Gary got it. When she finds out it belongs to me, maybe she'll make him give it back." He jumped up again. "Come on. Let's go talk to her."

"Reuben, wait . . . maybe we should wait until Gary's not home. If he sees us talking to his mother . . . . "

"No. I don't care if he sees us or not. He already knows we want the watch. And I can't wait any longer. I have to get my watch, don't you see that?"

"Of course. I know that but, but . . . . "

"Look, Jessie, you don't have to come. You've already done more for me than I can ever repay you for. But I can't wait. The thought of him with my watch is driving me out of my mind. I can't think about anything but getting it back. I'll do whatever I have to do to get it back."

I knew he meant what he said. "Okay. Let's go. She knows me, so it'll be easier if I come too."

We walked up the beach toward the Richtors' house. When we got closer I saw that the car was in the driveway, which meant that Mrs. Richtor was home. There was no sign of Gary and the dog. Maybe he was still out, farther up the beach, or maybe he was in the house. I hoped he was out.

We walked to the Richtors' front door and I pressed the doorbell. In a minute Mrs. Richtor appeared. She was an overweight woman dressed in pink stretch pants and a bright flowery blouse. Her black hair was teased high into an elaborate hairdo and she wore glasses that had gold-sequined, butterfly-wing frames. "Yes?" she said, standing in the doorway.

Reuben was staring at her, and I realized that he had probably never seen glasses like that. To me she looked silly and kind of pathetic, but Reuben didn't know what to make of her. I said, "Uh, I'm Jessie Cameron, your neighbor? And this is my cousin Reuben Miller."

"Oh, yes. Hello there, Jessie. I expect you're here to see Gary?"

"Well, actually, we wanted to talk to you about something."

"Oh. You must be selling something. Girl Scout cookies? A raffle?"

"N-not exactly. Actually . . ." I wasn't sure what to say. I couldn't just come right out and accuse her son of stealing a watch. I looked at Reuben.

"Umm, yes," he said, "I, ah, I'm missing my watch. It was my grandfather's pocket watch. It's most awfully important to me . . . and umm, I wondered if . . . well, actually, Jessie saw Gary with it, and we wondered if we could get it back."

Mrs. Richtor stood blinking in confusion. She looked at me. "You saw my Gary with your cousin's watch?"

Reuben replied for me, "I lost it, you see, and we think Gary may have found it. I just want to get it back."

"I see. You think Gary found your watch. Well, let me just call him." She went to the stairs and called "Gary, dear. Some friends of yours are here."

"Huh?"

"Come down here please, dear. There's someone to see you."

In a minute Gary came lumbering down the steps. When he saw us, he said, "What are you two doing here?"

"They were wondering if you'd seen a watch, dear. This young man has lost his and they thought perhaps you might have—"

"I told you I ain't seen yer bloody watch. Understand?" He glared at us from the stairs.

"Now, Gary dear. I'm sure they didn't mean any—"

"Shut up, Ma," he interrupted her before she could finish, and, taking two lumbering steps from the stairs to the door, he pushed his mother aside, grabbed the door, and slammed it in our faces.

We stood there on the steps for a minute, staring at the closed door. Then we looked at each other. I shrugged. "Well, we tried. I told you it was useless."

"Now what?" asked Reuben as we turned and went down the walk, back toward my yard.

"We'll have to sneak into his house and get it. There's no other way."

"But what about his parents? I don't see how we can just walk into the house and take back my watch. It's not going to be that easy."

"Whoever said it was going to be easy? All I said was it's the only way."

We went back down to the beach and sat down on the sand. Reuben scooped sand over his bare feet, and then shook it off. He looked at me. "Do you have a plan?"

"Well, I guess the first thing we have to do is watch the house and wait until they're all out." From where we were sitting on the beach, we could still see the back of the Richtors' house and the car parked in the driveway.

"But don't they lock it? How are we going to get in?"

"See that window right there? The one on the left, facing this way?"

Reuben nodded, looking up at the house. "That's Gary's room. I've seen him climb out at night. He climbs out into that tree and then climbs down. I've seen him go back in the same way. And if he can do it, why can't we?"

"Well, I suppose we can try. But what if someone sees us?"

"One of us can be a lookout, and one of us can go in. If anyone comes, well, it's a chance we have to take."

"All right. I'll go in, and you can be the lookout."

I nodded. That seemed fair to me. I mean, after all, it was his watch, and I have to admit I didn't exactly relish the idea of prowling around Gary Richtor's bedroom looking for it.

"There's just one problem." Reuben said.

"What?"

"What if he keeps the watch with him? Most people do, you know."

The thought had crossed my mind too, but we had to start somewhere. "Well, Gary's not most people. He might have buried it in the backyard for all we know, but his room is the most logical place to start."

We watched the house the rest of the afternoon, waiting for an opportunity to sneak into Gary's room, but the car stayed in the drive all day. Finally when the sun was going down and the air was getting colder we left the beach.

# 15

IT WAS FOUR O'CLOCK the next day when we finally got our chance. We had been watching from the window in my room, and getting more and more impatient. "What'll we do if they don't go out for the rest of the day? I've got school tomorrow. I won't be home until four, and Gary gets home the same time I do. What's wrong with them? Don't they have any friends? Don't they ever go out?"

"Wait," Reuben said, "She's coming out of the house with her purse. And he's right behind her. They're—yes—they're getting in the car."

I jumped up and ran to the window. Gary's parents were getting into the car. As we watched, they started the car, backed out of the driveway, and drove off down the street.

"Come on. Now's our chance. Gary's out on his bike. The house is empty. It's now or never."

"But what if he comes back?" Reuben asked.

"It's a chance we've got to take. We may not get another before Mom comes home. You want your watch, don't you?" I said as I led him downstairs.

He followed me outside, across our backyard, and into the Richtors'. When we reached the tree just below the window, Reuben said, "You're sure that's Gary's window?"

I nodded. "And it's open. It's always open."

"All right. You keep watch. I'll go in." He took a deep breath and heaved himself up onto the first limb of the tree. He climbed slowly and steadily, while I waited nervously on the ground below the tree, jumping at every sound I heard. In a few minutes he disappeared inside, then, once he was in, returned to wave to me, just to let me know he was okay.

I stood there, staring up at the open window as though it were a big open mouth that had swallowed him up. Every few minutes I checked on either side of the house to make sure no one was coming. Five minutes passed, then ten. What was taking him so long? Maybe he'd gotten his head stuck under the bed and was strangling to death, or maybe someone was in the house and Reuben was trapped, hiding in the closet. I was imagining all kinds of horrible possibilities when he leaned out the window.

"Any luck?" I called up to him.

He shook his head. "He must be wearing it. I've searched every drawer in his room, every shelf. It's not here."

A movement up the street caught my eye, and I ran around the side of the house to see what it was. When I saw Gary pedaling toward the house I almost screamed. I ran back and called softly up to Reuben. "Come down, quick! He's coming. I'll stall him to give you time to get down."

"Oh, my," Reuben said, scrambling out the window.

I walked around the front of the house, trying to look cool and calm, and waved for Gary to stop before he rode down the driveway.

He rode up, hitting the brakes suddenly so that a spray of dirt and sand flew up and stung my legs. Typical.

"What do you want?" he asked.

"I'm looking for a cat. Have you seen one?" I asked.

"A cat? When did you get a cat?"

"We didn't, but Dana, you know my friend, Dana, she has one, and it's missing. I'm just helping her look for it."

I could see something gold sticking out of the top of his pocket. It was the watch. He saw what I was looking at and shoved it farther into his pocket.

"There's no cat around here. I know what you're look-ing for. But you won't get it. And you can tell that to your weirdo friend. I know who he is. I saw him on the beach that day."

Then he got this really creepy look on his face and he reached over and touched my hair with his dirty sausage-like fingers. I slapped his hand away hard, and fought the urge to turn and run. I wasn't going to let him think I was scared of him. "Don't you dare touch me. Don't you ever touch me again. Do you understand?"

He held his hands up, palms out. "Hey, lighten up, babe."

I turned and walked away, pretending to look for Dana's cat, but as soon as I got into my own yard I started to run. Reuben was waiting for me on the back steps.

"Whew! That was close. Are you all right?" Reuben said when he saw me.

"Yeah, I'm okay." I caught my breath and added, "I just hate him, that's all. He's got the watch in his pocket. I saw part of the chain."

Reuben nodded. "It wasn't in his room. I figured he had to have it on him."

"Now what?" I said.

Reuben was quiet, thinking.

"You have an idea, don't you?" I asked him.

"I think there's only one thing left . . . ," he started to say, then he stopped and shook his head. "No. Never mind. It's nothing."

Daphne came out and sat on the steps with us then, and we couldn't talk about it anymore. But later that night, just before we went to bed, I said to Reuben, "So. What now? I have to go to school tomorrow, and I won't be home until four. What are you going to do?"

"Don't worry. I'll be all right."

That was all I could get out of him, but I was pretty sure he had a plan. So I wasn't all that surprised when something woke me in the middle of the night. I looked at my clock. 2:30 A.M. Though it was late, it was a clear night, and the light of the moon shone in my window, casting an eerie silvery glow over my room. I lay still for a minute, listening and thinking, and then I heard the creak of the stairs, and I knew right away who it was. I got up and quickly pulled on a pair of jeans and a sweater and tiptoed out of my room and down the stairs. I caught up with Reuben just as he was about to go out the back door. "Reuben, wait," I said, just loud enough for him to hear.

I startled him and he spun around quickly, "Jessie. What are you doing up?"

"I just woke up. I heard you on the steps, and I knew where you were going. Why didn't you wake me?" I crossed the kitchen to where he stood by the back door. "Let's go outside so we don't wake Daphne and Will," I said. I took my parka from where it hung on its hook by the back door and slid into it, and we went out into the night. "You're going to get the watch, aren't you?" I said.

He nodded.

"Why didn't you wake me?" I asked him again.

"Jessie—" he began.

"If you think you're going over there without me, you're wrong," I told him.

"Look, there's no point in both of us going. It's too risky. If he wakes up . . . ."

"Reuben, I'm going with you. There's nothing more to say."

"All right, but I'm going in by myself, like yesterday. There's no point in both of us going in. We'll only make more noise if there are two of us."

It was true. There was less chance of waking Gary if only one of us went in. "Okay. I'll wait at the bottom of the tree, like yesterday."

It was cold as we walked across our yard to the Richtors'. I shivered and pulled my parka tighter around me. Reuben was wearing his sweatshirt, and his hands were jammed into the pockets of his jeans. "Aren't you freezing?" I asked him as a gust of wind blew off the river.

"Yes, I guess I am," he said as if he hadn't really thought about it.

We came to the oak tree and we both stopped and looked up at Gary's window looming above us, a black hole in the white wall of the house.

"Well, here goes," he said, and he swung himself up onto the lower branch of the tree and started climbing. In a minute he had reached the window and hoisted himself in, turning to wave as he had done yesterday. Again, I stood on the ground below, staring up at the window, but this time I knew that Gary was in there asleep. At least, I hoped he was asleep. "Don't let him wake up. Please God, don't let him wake up," I whispered over and over to myself.

Each minute seemed like an hour as I stood there, waiting, wondering what would happen if Gary did wake up. How would we explain it if he woke his parents? I mean, if you're caught snooping around someone's room in the middle of the night, what are you going to say—"Oh, hi. We just came up for a visit"? Even the Richtors wouldn't buy that. So I'm standing there getting more and more worried when finally I see Reuben in the window. He climbs out onto the tree branch and in a minute he's beside me, holding the watch. I almost screamed I was so happy, but instead I grabbed him and hugged him. "You got it!" I whispered. "I don't believe it."

"Shhh. Let's get out of here," he said, and he took my hand and we ran back over to my yard.

"I got it," Reuben said, as soon as we were out of the Richtors' yard. He held the watch up. "You don't know how happy I am to see this."

We went up the back steps and on into our kitchen. I turned on the light, and we sat down at the kitchen table. "You don't know how happy I am that we don't have to explain what you were doing sneaking around Gary's bedroom. What happened? Was he asleep the whole time?"

Reuben nodded. "Snoring away. The only problem was I couldn't find it. I searched the top of his bureau, his desk, and everywhere. Then it hit me that it was probably still in his pants pocket. I started looking for his pants, and finally found them under the bed. I was really scared he was going to wake up when I looked under there, but I got them, and there it was. He hadn't even bothered to take it out of his pants."

Reuben put the watch on the table and I picked it up and looked at it closely. It was beautiful. More beautiful than I had imagined. The cover was engraved gold and there was a little button you pushed to open it. The face was a painting: a painting of a ship sailing on the sea, and on one side of the sea was the sun, and on the other, the moon. What was amazing was the way the colors blended into each other, from the reds and oranges of the sunrise, to the light blue of the noonday sky, and finally into the violet and indigo of the night sky. I stared at the painting for a long time. "I didn't know it would be so . . . beautiful," I said. "It's a ship sailing through time, isn't it?"

"You know, I never really thought about it like that, but, yes, I suppose that's exactly what it is."

"What do you think Gary will do when he finds it's gone?" I asked.

"He'll know we took it, but it's mine. What can he do? Anyway, I don't plan to stick around to find out. If I'm gone you can pretend you knew nothing about it. He can't prove you had anything to do with it."

"Yeah. So, you're going? Just like that?" I said.

It was funny, but all of a sudden I didn't want him to go. It would be so final. I mean, he wasn't just going to another city or another state. He was going to another century.

Reuben pushed his hair back out of his eyes. He looked at me and then looked down at the table. "Jessie, I've been gone a week now, and it feels like years. I've got to get home. It's been . . . strange, being here. So much has happened, and I've seen so much. I'll never be the same again, I know that."

"Me either," I said.

There was a noise on the stairs, and Will appeared in the doorway of the kitchen.

"Why are you guys up?" he asked.

"Come here, Willy," I said. "Take a look at this." I showed him the watch. He took it in his hands and studied it.

"Wow!" he said when he saw the inside. "How did you get it back?"

"Reuben went into Gary's room and took it. There was no other way," I told him.

Will nodded. "So now what?"

"Now, I have to be going. I've been away a long time, and I miss my home. I miss my parents and my friends. It's time I was getting back," Reuben told him.

Will nodded. "Will we ever see you again?" he asked Reuben.

"I don't know for sure, but I think so. I'll always have the watch, and maybe sometime I'll come back. Remember, I won't be gone. I'll just be living in a different time."

Will was quiet, thinking. "Jessie, do you think that's the way it is with Dad?"

"Of course, Willy. We know that now." I took Will's hand and held it.

Reuben watched us. "You don't remember your father, do you, Will?"

Will shook his head. "I was only two when he died. I've tried and tried, but I can't remember."

Reuben pursed his lips, staring at the watch. He seemed to be trying to make up his mind about something. Finally he said, "Would you like to see him? Just once, I mean. We could go back, just so you could see him. Just for a few minutes." He looked at me. "I . . . I owe you both so much. I'd like to do something for you."

"You mean, go back through time . . . back to when he was alive?"

"Just for a few minutes. Would you like that?"

I thought for a minute. To see my father, alive . . . even for just a few minutes. "Yes. Yes, I would like that."

Will looked at me. "If I saw him again, then I'll have something to remember."

I nodded. "Wait here a minute," I said. I left the kitchen and ran upstairs to my bedroom. I opened the bottom drawer of my desk and took out the photograph of my father and me. There was a date on the back: August 20, 1988. It had been taken just a couple of weeks before he died. I took it back downstairs and showed it to Reuben. "I want to go back to this day," I said, handing him the picture. "August 20, 1988."

# 16

REUBEN SET THE WATCH for August 20, 1988. "What time?" he asked.

I shrugged. "Around noon, I guess."

He set it for noon. "I need some water and some matches." I went to the sink and filled a glass with water and put it on the table in front of him. "Is this all right?" I asked.

He nodded.

Then I opened the drawer next to the stove and took out a box of kitchen matches. "Anything else?"

He shook his head. "But we had better go up to your room. Somewhere we know no one else will be. If your mother or someone is in the kitchen . . . "

I nodded. I could imagine what would happen if the three of us just popped into the kitchen. What would Mom do? I didn't want to find out. And then it hit me, what we were about to do. What if something went wrong? What if we couldn't get back, or what if we went to the wrong time? "Reuben, are you sure . . ."

"Come on. You don't want to back out now, do you?"

Will looked at me. "Do you, Jessie?"

I didn't say anything, just sat there with Reuben and Will staring at me, waiting to see what I was going to say. It was so quiet I could hear the watch ticking. I knew I had to make a decision. I wanted to try it, but I was scared. I was scared not only at the thought of traveling through time, but also at what I might learn. I knew, somehow, that once we did it, once we traveled through time, I would never be the same again. I would be changed, for better or worse, and nothing would ever seem quite the same to me again. Did I want to change?

Finally Will said, "Jessie?" and I knew it was too late to turn back. "Let's go," I said, and the three of us stood up, and, taking the matches and the glass of water, we went upstairs to my room.

We sat on the floor in a circle. Reuben put the watch in the middle. "Everyone's got to be touching the watch," he said.

Will and I held onto the watch chain. "Everyone ready?" Reuben asked. We nodded, and Reuben lit a match. "Jessie, I'm going to touch the watch with the match. Sprinkle a few drops of water over it when I do."

He held the watch with one hand, and brought the match to it with the other. When the flame touched the face of the watch, I sprinkled water over it. The face of the watch began to glow, and the painting seemed to come to life. The sea began to move, and the ship looked as if it were really sailing. The stars, the moon, and the sun glowed with their own light. I reached for Will's hand just as the painting began to swallow us up . . . I could feel the spray from the sea, and the rocking of the waves. Everything seemed to be swirling, hundreds of colors, all jumbled together, and I felt as if I was being pulled through space. With one hand I held onto the watch chain, and with the other I held onto Will. I couldn't tell if my eyes were open or closed, and I had no idea how much time had passed. Then, the swirling seemed to slow, and the face of the watch came back into focus. And we were sitting on the floor in my room, just as we had been, but it was different. My old wallpaper was on the walls, and the noonday sun streamed through my open window. I looked at Will and Reuben. They looked just the same as they had, except they both looked dazed, as if they had just woken up.

"I think we're here," said Reuben "1988."

A warm breeze blew through the window. I could hear birds singing, and insects humming. Summer. August. I stood up and went to the window. I saw the same view that I see every day of my life, but there were little tiny differences. The pine trees down by the shore were smaller, and the toolshed was painted tan instead of green. And down on the dock I saw him, my father . . . . Though he was far away I knew without a doubt that it was him. I would have known him anywhere, the familiar way he leaned over the piling, pulling in the line, ready to catch a crab. A rush of warm feeling surged through me, a feeling of love and safeness that I hadn't felt for years, since . . . since the day he had died. I beckoned to Will. "There he is, Willy. On the dock." Will came to stand beside me and looked out the window. "See him?" I asked. Will looked and then nodded, but he didn't say anything. I put my arm around him, and we stood in the window watching our father net a crab.

I looked at Reuben. "Can we go outside?" I asked.

He nodded. "But don't let him see you. We can hide in that little group of pines down near the shore."

We tiptoed downstairs, checking to make sure there was no one around to see us. "The car's gone. Mom must be out," I said, as we passed the driveway. We ran across the lawn to the pine trees, and from there we had a perfect view of the dock.

"There's our little rowboat. We used to play in it for hours, Will."

And there in the boat I saw a girl and a little boy. The girl was about nine and wore a blue and red bathing suit. The little boy wore an orange life jacket and sat in the middle seat, his short legs sticking out in front of him. It took me a minute to realize it was Will and me.

"That's us, Will. We used to play in that boat all the time. We weren't allowed to go out in it, but Dad would let us sit in it while he fished or crabbed if it was tied up to the dock."

"Yeah, I . . . I think I remember that, sort of. The bottom of the boat was painted green, right?"

"Right. And it was peeling, and you used to peel the paint off and throw it in the water. You thought that was really a fun thing to do."

As we watched, Dad put the net down and said, "Well, I guess the crabs are taking a siesta. Maybe it's a good time for us to go in and get some lunch." He took a handkerchief out of the back pocket of his pants and mopped his face. Then he pulled the rope that held the rowboat. "Who wants a hotdog?"

"Me," shouted the two-year-old Will, holding his hands up to Dad to be lifted out of the boat. Dad leaned down and plucked him off the seat and pulled him up, swinging him high into the air. "All that seafaring makes a man hungry, huh?" he said, swinging Will down and holding him against his hip with one hand while he held out his other for me. But I ignored the hand and hoisted myself up onto the dock without my father's help. I walked to the piling on the end of the dock and pulled on the crab line. "There's something on this one, Dad," I called, reaching for the net. "Can I net it?"

"Okay. Let's see what you can do," he said, standing a few feet behind with Will.

I watched myself take the net and with my other hand pull the line in. I made a quick, practiced scoop, and brought a big blue crab out of the water. "I got him," I said proudly, holding the net up so my father could inspect the catch.

"Not bad. Take him and put him in the bucket with the others," he said.

The nine-year-old me walked up the dock to where the bucket of crabs sat in the shade of the locust trees on shore, and flipped the crab out of the net into the bucket. My father and Will came up and the three of us peered into the bucket, watching the crabs scrambling. "Ornery creatures, aren't they?" my father said. He let his hand rest on my neck, and then the three of us walked across the lawn and disappeared into the house.

Reuben and Will and I sat quietly. No one spoke until finally I said, "Two weeks later he died in the accident."

"But we didn't know that then," said Will.

"No," I said.

"I'm glad," said Will.

"Me too."

I looked at the house, our house. It looked pretty much the same, except the trim was white then instead of gray, and the trees and bushes around it were smaller. So much had changed in those four years, and yet so much was the same. Part of me wanted to run into the house and fling myself on my father, and hug him as though I would never have another chance, because of course, I wouldn't. But I knew I couldn't do that now. The three of them were inside, and the thought of the three of them in there, happily eating their lunch, made me feel good. I don't know why, but I felt peaceful and happy, and as though I had seen what we had come to see.

"Are you ready to go back now?" Reuben asked us.

We nodded together. Reuben set the watch for 1992, reached into his pocket and took out the matches. I got some water from the river and sprinkled it over the watch face. Reuben lit the match and held it to the watch, and once again the ship came to life and the colors began to swirl. The next thing I knew we were sitting outside in the dark, beneath the same group of pine trees. I was shivering."Brr. It's not August anymore. Let's go inside."

We stood up and ran together across the lawn and into the warmth of the kitchen.

# 17

BACK IN THE KITCHEN, everything was just as we had left it. Even the hands on the clock had hardly moved at all. Will and Reuben sat at the table, and I put some milk on the stove to make hot chocolate. When the milk was hot I made the hot chocolate and brought the mugs to the table. Reuben warmed his hands on the mug and then took a sip. "What will you tell Daphne when she finds I'm gone in the morning?" he asked.

"I'll just tell her you had to catch an early bus. She'll believe it," I said.

"Will you be glad to see your parents?" Will asked.

Reuben nodded. "I never thought I'd admit it, but I will be glad to see them. I miss home. It's been . . ." he shook his head, "strange. But I'm glad it happened. If it hadn't, I . . . never would have met you."

"Do you think . . . maybe you'll come back sometime?" I asked. All of a sudden I didn't want to lose him. The thought that I might never see him again was awful.

He nodded. "I'd like to come back. I guess I shouldn't make any promises, because you never know what might happen, but I'll try. Maybe next year, around the same time."

"Not for a whole year?" said Will. "Why don't you come back at Halloween. You can go trick-or-treating with us."

Reuben laughed. "That sounds great, Will, but I don't think I'll be ready for another trip by then. I've got things to do at home, and this time traveling, it's . . . confusing. I don't think I can do it too often."

We finished our hot chocolate and then Reuben picked up the watch. "Well, I guess it's about that time." He twisted the dials, setting the date and the time. When he was done he laid it down on the table again. He looked at me and brushed his hair out of his eyes. "Um. I don't know what to say. I hate saying good-bye."

"I know. Me too."

"I'd tell you I'll write, but . . ."

"Even if you could you'd probably forget," I said.

"I will come back, though. I really will."

I nodded. "I know."

And then, before either of us could say any more he lit a match, sprinkled some water on the watch, and vanished right before our eyes.

At first the kitchen felt empty, but as I looked around me I thought how good everything looked, everything . . . all the little tiny things that make up our house and our life, they all looked good. The way Will's pictures from school were hung on the refrigerator, and the way the moonlight shone on the bench by the window. The way Mom's books were stacked on the counter, and even the way Eric's jacket was hung on the hook by the back door.

It was weird, but something had happened to me when we went back in time. I didn't know what it was, and I still don't really, and I guess it was just that I had learned something. It's hard to put into words, but I guess I learned that we each get our own little bit of time, just a tiny bit, a few drops of water in the whole ocean. And those drops are part of the whole ocean, but they're ours too, and we can do whatever we want with them. I guess I learned that those drops are pretty special, and I didn't want to waste mine.

"Do you think he'll come back?" Will asked.

"I think so. But not for a while." I stood up. "Come on, Willy. We better get to bed before Daphne wakes up. Anyway, I've had it."

I put the mugs in the sink and followed Will up to his room. He took my hand. "Come in for a minute," he said. He climbed into bed and pulled the covers up to his chin. I sat down on the bed beside him. "I remember Dad, now," he told me.

I nodded. "I'm glad."

"Me too."

"Jessie?"

"What."

"I'm glad Mom's going to marry Eric."

"I know."

"Are you?"

"I don't know if I'm glad, but I'm happy for Mom. It'll work out, Willy. It'll be different, but it'll work out."

"Yeah." He shut his eyes and I thought he was about to go to sleep when he sat bolt upright. "Jessie!"

"What?"

"He forgot his clothes. Reuben forgot his clothes."

The brown paper bag that had Reuben's oilskins, knickers, and his lace-up boots was sitting on Will's extra bed.

"Night, Willy," I said.

"Night, Jessie." I kissed his forehead and crossed the hall to my own room. As I got into my own bed I wondered how Reuben was going to explain his new clothes to his parents. Well, anyway, I thought, next time he comes back he can wear the jeans instead of his own dorky clothes.

And he will come back. Someday he will come back.